Also by John Morsell:

Death at the End of the Road

In this first of the Charlie Skyler mystery series, Charlie and his quirky friends find themselves embroiled in an intrigue involving several murders, an eccentric drug lord, mysterious government agents, and psychopathic assassins. The unique coastal Alaskan town of Homer provides the back drop for their various adventures as they play detective and, at the same time, defend themselves against vengeful members of a widespread drug distribution ring with roots in the Vietnam War.

Five Star Chanticleer Review
for
Death at the End of the Road

"A delightful suspense with splashes of humor, and some romance, "Death at the End of the Road" is a book you won't want to miss, especially if you yearn to live vicariously through characters of nontraditional lifestyles and appreciate the natural scenery of one of the most beautiful places in the US."

–CHANTICLEER REVIEWS

THE
RARE EARTH
MURDERS

A Charlie Skyler Alaskan Mystery

John Morsell

ISBN: 978-0-578-33565-0
Library of Congress Control Number: 2021923648
Cover Design by @ Kathleen Weisel
Book Design by © Rachel Johnson

Printed by Village Books Publishing

First printing edition 2022

Village Books
1200 11th Street
Bellingham, WA 98225

In memory of Ann and Scott.

Author's Introduction

The town of Homer on Alaska's Kenai Peninsula and the surrounding Lower Cook Inlet environs are, of course, real places. I have tried to describe the geographical, ecological, and historical aspects of the area accurately throughout the book. I assume full responsibility for any inaccuracies that may occur. It should be noted, however, that *The Rare Earth Murders* is a work of fiction, and, as such, some of the specific locations and circumstances integral to the plot are just plain made up. I apologize to any persons familiar with the area if this juxtaposition of real and unreal causes confusion or consternation.

THE
RARE EARTH
MURDERS

A Charlie Skyler Alaskan Mystery

John Morsell

Cast of Characters

Charlie Skyler: a boat-dwelling ecotour guide whose curiosity often leads to impromptu, if unhealthy, detective work

Kate Perkins: a swamp-dwelling Midwest transplant who gets sucked into Charlie's intrigues

Johann Sebastian Bachman (JB): an enigmatic retired hippie academic with special skills and a mysterious background

Bob Stillwater (Super Trooper): an enthusiastic Alaska State Trooper

Beverly Milford: a junior DEA agent with a bulldog mentality, love of Alaska, and infatuation with JB

Jeremy Franks: a young geologist prospecting for gold at a claim on Cook Inlet; partner in a consulting company, South Peninsula Gold (SPG)

Jason Biele: Jeremy's partner at SPG, also a geologist

Janine Franks: Jeremy's sister and administrator at SPG

Dr. Mort French: a medical examiner, forensic pathologist

...continued on next page

...continued from previous page

Julie Quantrell: a wildlife biologist

Craig Johnson: a mining engineer for Northwest Base Metals (NBM) Consortium

Bryce Cameron: a clueless investor in NBM project

Max Karelian: a mysterious security guy for NBM

Joel Spurgeon: a junior geologist at NBM

Hank Gottfried: an NBM executive from Vancouver

Lee Chen: a mysterious Chinese backer of NBM project

Travis Chen: Lee Chen's nephew; foreman of mineral exploration core drilling effort

Ed Jackson: a professor of minerology

Chapter One

Charlie Skyler had awakened with a bad feeling. He was expecting a call from the geologists confirming their pickup time, but there had been only silence. Something was seriously wrong. Plus, he was running late. The Shearwater plowed through the milky water of Cook Inlet fighting the unusually high tide. The current was, of course, running the wrong way. To make matters worse, the amount of debris in the water demanded that he periodically slow to an idle and thread his way between the logs and rafts of kelp. Flotsam and jetsam tended to concentrate in areas – locally known as rip lines – where saline marine water collided with lower density fresh water from the many rivers emptying into the estuary. In some areas there were whole trees floating amidst the usual assortment of plastic water bottles and chunks of Styrofoam. He could not afford to hit a log or run over seaweed that might clog his engine's cooling intake.

Jeremy Franks had called via satellite phone the week before to arrange for a pickup from their remote camp on the west side of Cook Inlet. He sounded relaxed and excited about their preliminary investigations into the potential for a gold find on their new claim. Charlie emphasized that they needed to be packed and ready to go so that the transfer from land to boat could be as quick as possible.

After a long four hours, Charlie finally reached the west side. He drove the Shearwater to within a hundred feet of shore, sounded his horn, and dropped the anchor. He carefully backed down to make sure that the anchor was deeply embedded in the sea bottom and turned off his engine. He noticed that it was just too quiet — even the gulls had stopped their incessant racket. The current was starting to pick up on the rising tide — not what he wanted to see. Anchoring in this location with its strong current and poor holding ground was problematic, and he was not anxious to leave the boat to the mercy of Cook Inlet's extreme tides. As the swirling current pulled the boat against the taught anchor line, Charlie's eyes scanned the shoreline. The two geologists were supposed to be waiting with their gear ready to load. The lack of movement on shore intensified his earlier uneasiness and caused his gut to clench. He would have to go ashore and see what was going on.

Charlie launched the dinghy with its small outboard off of the back deck of the Shearwater. He clipped the portable marine radio to his belt and slung his shotgun over his shoulder. He carefully lowered his six-foot one-inch body into the tiny rubber craft and started the motor. The day was oppressive with a low overcast sky, high humidity and no wind. He could almost feel the barometer dropping.

He smelled it as soon as the dinghy grounded on the small beach. Knowing that the tide was rapidly rising, Charlie carefully tied the dinghy to a tree. He unslung the gun, chambered a shell, and walked ashore into the small camp under the spruce trees. The last time he had been there, the camp had been neat with a central fire hearth, portable camp table, and tents on each side. A blue tarp awning had covered the cooking area, creating a cozy camp atmosphere. But now it was a mess. Both tents and the tarp were knocked down and crumpled. Garbage and personal belongings were scattered everywhere. A large pile of bear crap brought several thoughts to mind – none of them good. At best, the bear had chased the geologists away and wrecked their camp; at worst, the bear had attacked and killed the geologists. Unfortunately, the pervasive smell suggested the latter. Charlie's breakfast attempted an escape. He fired the shotgun once into the air in hopes that any bears would retreat. The gun-shot seemed incredibly loud in the still air, the sound reverberating off the mountainsides like thunder.

Charlie moved to the right side of the natural clearing under the tall spruce and into the underbrush. Out of the corner of his eye he saw a lumpy mass on the ground. Before he was close enough to make it out, he knew what it was. The partially consumed carcass of Jeremy Franks was spread-eagled on the ground. Running to the shore, Charlie threw up into the small waves lapping the beach and washed his mouth out with saltwater. *What the hell should he do now?* A brown bear protecting a kill is a very dangerous animal, and he had to get back to the Shearwater before the current got too strong for the anchor to hold. But Jeremy's partner, Jason Biele, was still missing.

Charlie yelled for Jason but got no response. There was still a chance that Jason was alive and lying injured somewhere. If that was the case, he needed to find him. Charlie began to walk the perimeter of the camp in ever widening circles. Bear sign was everywhere. He fired the gun again. As he approached the toe of the hillside behind the camp, he saw two ravens fly up into the trees from the dense brush. Shit, thought Charlie. He forced himself to walk in the birds' direction as they cackled in annoyance from the spruce branches overhead. Charlie reluctantly pushed aside the dense blueberry branches. He found Jason's mangled body partially covered with leaves and duff from the forest floor. Brown bears often return to a kill until it is fully consumed, and this bear was definitely going to return. In fact, the bear could be close by, sleeping in the bushes. *OK, this is enough, thought Charlie. I'm getting the hell out of here.*

Back in the Shearwater Charlie tried his mobile phone and found that the signal was weak but probably strong enough to call. He did not want to use the marine radio for such disturbing news. His first call was to Bob Stillwater, the Alaska State Trooper assigned to the southern Kenai Peninsula. Bob, affectionately known as the Super Trooper because of his enthusiasm in busting formerly illicit marijuana grow operations, had worked closely with Charlie in the past in the resolution of various criminal situations. The two were good friends, but Bob was reluctant to let Charlie get too involved because of professional liability and normal law enforcement practices. But, on the other hand, Bob knew that Charlie and his friends were smart and often contributed insights beyond his capability.

Since it was early afternoon and Charlie had a four-hour trip back to his home base in Homer on Kachemak Bay, it was decided that he would come back to the Homer harbor. Bob agreed to organize an investigation for the next day using a fast aluminum Trooper boat that could be beached at the site. Because of the steep, wooded terrain and lack of beach expanse, a helicopter would have no place to land. Bob's first job would be to assemble the appropriate team of people for the investigation, which at a minimum should include a wildlife biologist and the Peninsula Borough medical examiner.

Charlie's second call was to his friend and boat neighbor JB. JB had a number of special talents that Charlie felt could be useful in an investigation. Charlie informed JB that the whole situation was puzzling. A bear or bears had obviously been there, but it seemed unlikely that bears would have been able to kill both geologists without any warning; they were experienced Alaskans with bear protection weapons and satellite phone communication. It did not make sense. He had a bad feeling that something else was the cause of death and that the presence of bears was simply a result of the presence of available human carrion, which, while totally disgusting, was at least forgivable from the bear's standpoint. JB indicated a strong interest in the unpleasant situation and agreed to fit a morning expedition into his self-proclaimed busy schedule. If nothing else, JB was an excellent shot and could provide bear protection while everybody else looked around. "Oh," Charlie said into the phone. "Tell Kate I'll be late for dinner."

Charlie weighed anchor and headed back across Cook Inlet toward Homer. Because of the strong current, the Shearwater's heading was about 30 degrees south of the true bearing to compensate for sidewise movement. Fortunately, the GPS and autopilot performed the needed calculations and course adjustments so Charlie did not have to think about it. He had not done very well on the navigation questions in the test for his Coast Guard license. Plus he was not in the mood to deal with charts and vector algebra.

The town of Homer is located in south-central Alaska on the Kenai Peninsula, adjacent to the north side of Kachemak Bay, a long, narrow body of water that adjoins Lower Cook Inlet. The city of Anchorage is about seventy-five miles north of Homer as the crow flies, but the highway connection between the two towns is two hundred twenty-five miles long because of inconveniently located mountains and fjords.

As the Shearwater approached the wide entrance to Kachemak Bay, the low-lying Homer spit where the harbor is located was still not visible because of the earth's curvature. Approaching closer, the taller buildings at the end of the six-mile long spit began to appear like a disconnected mirage floating in the air in the middle of the bay. Closer still, the strange projection into the marine environment began to take shape, extending to its full length and connecting with higher mainland terrain.

Forty-five minutes later the Shearwater turned into the harbor entrance on the back side of the spit. All Charlie had been able to think about on the long boring trip across the bay was Jason's partially eaten corpse. While he had not known Jason and Jeremy well, they were likeable young men with contagious enthusiasm. They were both recent graduates of the University of Alaska College of Engineering and Mines and were excited about putting their knowledge to use. They had pooled their money to purchase a mining claim that nobody else wanted, hoping that it might be profitable or, at least, provide some experience. Unfortunately, their Alaskan adventure had come to a horrible end.

†

"I guess you've had a bad day," Kate said while catching the stern line as Charlie maneuvered the Shearwater into his narrow slip in the Homer harbor. Her lithe dancer's body moved effortlessly across the dock.

"That's an understatement to say the least. You must have talked to JB."

"Yeah. I just spent the last two hours consoling Janine. She's in kind of bad shape." Janine, Jeremy's sister, was also the secretary, general administrator, and gofer for South Peninsula Gold. SPG was a small geological consulting company that Jeremy and Jason had set up to make some money consulting for others, as well as to pursue exploration on their gold claim.

"You look terrible, Charlie," said Kate as she hugged her large boyfriend.

"I'm feeling a little better than I did before. My stomach did some major loops when I saw the bodies. I'm hoping I won't ever have to see anything like that again, at least until tomorrow when we go back there."

A gangly, long-haired apparition jumped from a rickety nearby sailboat and helped to tie up the Shearwater. "You're looking a little green there buddy."

"Thanks, JB. You always know just the right things to say."

The three friends assembled in the cabin of Charlie's boat. Kate and JB waited for Charlie to tell his story. "Care for a beer?" asked JB.

"Thanks for the generous offer, especially since it's my refrigerator, but I think I'll pass until my stomach quiets down. The gist of my unfortunate adventure is that Jeremy and Jason are dead and bears have torn up the campsite along with the bodies. It was a very creepy scene, and I didn't stay very long."

"What do you think happened?" Kate asked.

"Unless there was a whole herd of bears, it doesn't seem likely that the guys were killed by the animals. They were too experienced, and they would have made sure to minimize leaving stuff around that would have attracted bears. But decomposing bodies would have attracted bears from miles around. Whatever happened was pure evil. Hopefully, an investigation will shed some light on the situation."

"Do you really need to go back there?" asked Kate.

"Yeah, I do. Meanwhile, Kate, if Janine feels up to it, maybe you can talk to her while we're gone tomorrow. See if she has any ideas why they might have been killed. I'd be especially interested whether they had contacts from other prospectors or mining companies about their claim. Bob will want to talk to her eventually, but he's going to be busy dealing with bodies and the crime scene for a while."

"OK. I can do that."

Chapter Two

At nine o'clock the next morning a beefy aluminum boat with a small cabin and two humongous outboard motors pulled up to the shore along the west side of Lower Cook Inlet where Jeremy and Jason had been camped. The very fast boat had crossed the inlet from Homer in a little more than an hour. Aboard were Bob the Super Trooper, medical examiner Dr. Mort French, wildlife biologist Julie Quantrell, as well as Charlie and JB. Because of the shallow draft and bulletproof hull, they were able to pull up to shore and solidly ground the bow on the rocky beach. The investigation team reluctantly climbed out onto the narrow intertidal zone. Julie fired her shotgun twice to warn any bears that might be around. No bears were visible, but very fresh scat piles were all over the place, one of which contained a brass button with a jeans logo. Charlie fought against nausea and noticed that aside from Mort and JB, the others were having similar difficulties.

The small group gathered on shore and discussed strategy. "Jeremy's body is located over there at the edge of the bushes," said Charlie as he pointed in the general direction.

"Mort, why don't you check out the body," suggested Bob. "JB, maybe you can go with him and watch for bears."

"Roger that," JB replied.

Mort, being accustomed to gruesome scenes, led the way to the first body. He was accompanied by JB, who served as both bear guard and informal consultant regarding unsavory matters.

Charlie gladly let the expert deal with the badly mutilated human remains and joined Julie and Bob as they searched the area for anything that might be useful in figuring out what might have happened. "Let's see if we can find any weapons that the geologists might have had to see if they were fired recently," said Bob as the group fanned out to canvass the former campsite.

"Hey Bob," Julie yelled from the camp perimeter. "I've got a gun."

"Leave it where it is. We'll be right there."

Bob and Charlie looked at the short-barreled pump action shotgun that was partly covered with dirt. Twelve-gauge shotguns loaded with lead slugs are the most popular bear protection weapon in Alaska because of their short-range stopping power. Bob photographed the gun in place, then picked it up, brushed off the dirt, opened the action and smelled the barrel. "It doesn't smell like it's been fired in the last few days and the magazine is full. I'm guessing that it wasn't used to fend off a bear attack. Looks like it was just scattered by the bear along with the rest of the camp stuff."

Just then Mort suddenly appeared like a ghost. He was holding a severed head and excitedly passing it from hand to hand like a basketball. Mort's naturally cadaverous appearance added to the creepy scene. Although some of the flesh was missing, the face was mostly intact and recognizable as Jeremy Franks.

"Christ, Mort," exclaimed Bob. "Not everyone here is used to this stuff. Do you think you could be a little more subtle? And aren't you supposed to be keeping the body in one piece?"

Mort, who was obviously in his element, looked excited. "Sorry. The head was already almost separated and I promise to return it to its proper place when we package things up. I thought you guys would like to see this." He held up Jeremy's head so that Bob and JB could see it. "There are obvious bullet holes in the skull – both an entry and an exit wound."

JB looked carefully as Julie hid behind the nearest tree and tried to control her gag reflex. One hole was just above the left eye and the other on the back of the skull. "Judging by the size of the entry hole and the relatively small amount of damage on exit, it looks like the wounds were from a moderately powered pistol bullet – maybe 9 mm. Also, the holes are lined up horizontally so, if Jeremy was standing at the time, then the shooter was probably also standing. Alternatively, if Jeremy was lying on the ground, the shooter would have had to fire straight down, a somewhat less likely scenario."

"I agree," said Mort.

Once again Charlie was amazed by JB's mysterious insight into all things violent and nefarious. Not for the first time, Charlie tried to imagine what kind of early education JB had received.

After Mort returned the head to its rightful location, Charlie led the way up the hill behind camp to Jason's body. The rest of the team followed closely. No one wanted to be left alone. "A bear or bears have been here since my visit yesterday," Charlie muttered. "The area is more trampled and there is more bear crap. I'm not going to look at the body again, so have at it, you guys."

Mort and JB approached the unpleasant mound on the forest floor. The body had been buried by the bear with enough cover material to reduce the scent and discourage other scavengers. After taking photos, they carefully scraped away the dirt and forest duff and made preliminary observations of the partially consumed remains. The corpse only vaguely resembled what it once had been.

Returning to the group that was standing just outside viewing range and upwind from the body, Mort said, "We were able to get a good look at the head and torso. No obvious head wounds, but the body is too mutilated to determine wounds to the soft tissues, at least until I get it back to my lab. But, Jason was wearing a belt holster with a .44 magnum revolver still strapped in. The pistol had not been fired. The hammer was resting on an empty chamber and the other five chambers contained unfired cartridges."

"Whatever happened to these guys had to have been a total surprise or else the intruders approached peacefully. Or maybe they were acquainted with the victims," JB said.

"Robbery doesn't seem like a likely motive since both guns were left behind. I suppose an alternative theory to double homicide might be murder-suicide, except it looks like neither of the guns was fired. And Jeremy's head wound definitely wasn't from a shotgun," added Bob. "Maybe we'll have a better idea when Mort does his autopsy."

"Has anybody seen any notes or files that might have been scattered around?" asked Charlie. "How about a satphone or other mobile phone?" The group frowned, but no one responded. Nothing seemed to make sense – or add up.

Mort and JB proceeded to package up the two bodies in body bags while the remainder of the team cleaned the site by bagging up all the camp debris. After the boat was loaded, the team explored a rough trail heading in a westerly direction. The trail, which apparently had been recently cleared by the geologists, followed a small, steep stream through dense spruce and hemlock along the base of the hillside, eventually heading uphill and breaking out onto alder-covered scree. The stream became a series of cascades and small falls descending a bedrock face. The trail continued up the steep slope, but hiking was difficult. Further exploration would have to wait for another day. The bodies needed to get back to town. As they were loading the boat, Julie noticed the satellite phone lying in about six inches of water on the shore. The phone was bagged along with the abandoned shotgun for return to Homer.

†

After helping to transfer the body bags from the trooper boat to Mort's hearse-like transport vehicle, Charlie and JB walked down the dock to the Shearwater's slip. Kate was waiting for them in the main salon. As usual, she was chowing down on a big bowl of potato chips with a beer chaser. "So Charlie, you look a little less green than you did yesterday."

"I guess I'm getting used to mutilated dead bodies. I think taking action to try and make sense of all this helps, not to mention getting the bodies out of the woods and away from the bears. I think I'd like a beer or two or three."

"Me too," said JB as he reached into Charlie's fridge and pulled out two microbrews.

"What did you find out from Janine?" said Charlie after briefing Kate on the day's events.

"She was very shook up, as you might expect. She said that Jeremy and Jason had met with, or rather were cornered by, a man who said he represented the owners of the mining claim immediately to the west of their claim. He tried to talk them into selling the claim and became somewhat belligerent when Jeremy suggested that they wanted to continue the exploration. The man's name was Hank Gottfried, and he worked for Northwest Base Metals Consortium, Ltd., a Canadian mining company. Janine has one of his cards. The company is apparently based in Vancouver. That was all she could think of that might be relevant to the murders. She has all the files for South Peninsula Gold in the office. She is okay with us reviewing them. I'm sure the authorities will also want to see them, so I suggested that she lock them up for now."

"I guess that might be a lead, although Gottfried would have to know that he would be the first suspect, assuming that he was involved," said JB.

"I Googled Northwest Base Metals and didn't find much of interest. It's a small company that specializes in exploring mineral prospects around the world and, if the minerals pan out, selling the prospects to large companies with the resources to permit and develop the mines. Their reputation seems to be OK, although I didn't see any indication that they had actually accomplished anything. I don't know much about corporate structure, but I think the company is owned by a small group of private investors who choose to remain anonymous. So guys, are we going to poke our noses into yet another violent mystery or are we going to do the smart thing and leave it up to the authorities?" added Kate.

"It seems like we've already started to poke," said JB. "We made such an awesome team on our last adventure it would be a shame to deprive the public of our services."

"Speaking of team members, have you heard anything from Beverly? Did she decide to quit the DEA?" asked Kate.

"She's going to come up here in about a week, and we're going to talk about it. If she moves up here from the lower forty-eight without any income, that will make two of us. Not a good formula for extravagant living."

Beverly was currently working out of the Los Angeles office of the Drug Enforcement Agency. She had worked with Charlie, Kate, and JB in the previous year when they had managed to dismantle a complex drug-distribution operation with key personnel living in Homer. Beverly and JB had fallen in love in spite of the fact that they were the most unlikely couple imaginable – DEA agent vs. hippie boat bum with a mysterious past.

"Well, I hope it works out for you guys," said Kate, always the romantic. "So, where do we go from here, as far as our dead guys are concerned?"

"It's probably best if we don't make ourselves too annoying to Bob," said Charlie. "He needs to take the lead. He took some flak from his superiors for involving civilians in the investigation after our last adventure. We will need to be more careful this time so he doesn't get into trouble — either clear things with him first or else be very sneaky and keep him in the dark. I suspect he will keep us in the loop if we don't piss him off."

"I would sure like to take a careful look at the claim property to see if that gives us any clues as to what Jeremy and Jason were looking at. Maybe we should schedule a day of hiking across the inlet. It seems like Bob wouldn't object to our taking a simple hike," suggested JB.

"Meanwhile we could get a better idea of the lay of the land by looking at claim boundaries, maybe superimposed on Google Earth imagery," said Charlie as he reached for another beer. "Plus, we can see whether Janine will let us look through the company files. The files probably contain maps of claim boundaries and maybe air photos. Right now we don't know anything about the value of the property, if any, or the ultimate motive for the killings. I suppose it's possible that the guys were killed by a wacko vagabond with no real motive, but that seems unlikely since valuable items like guns were left behind. Also, the missing notebooks and exploration logs suggest the motive may relate to mining."

Kate, being the most computer literate of the trio, had already pulled up the Google Earth image of the area on her laptop. "There's no need to wait for some of this information." She moved around the satellite image in the vicinity of the South Peninsula Gold property, trying various perspectives to get the best views.

"Look at this, guys. A pretty big mineral exploration operation has been underway on the claim next door."

A direct overhead aerial view showed the area of Jeremy and Jason's camp along with terrain to the west. A substantial semi-permanent camp could be seen seven miles west of the Cook Inlet shoreline. The presumed exploration camp consisted of four Quonset-like structures and a large square canvas tent, as well as cleared staging areas and a helicopter pad. The date on the imagery indicated that it had been updated about eight months earlier, so the exploration camp had been in place for at least that long.

Chapter Three

"I know Jeremy and Jason wanted to keep their prospecting results secret, but at this point those results may help us to understand why they were killed," said Kate as Janine reluctantly pulled the files from the company safe.

Janine sadly dumped several file folders on the small conference table in the SPG office. "I agree that it probably doesn't matter anymore. If it helps catch the killers I'm all for sharing. I guess I'm sort of the owner of the business now, such as it is. The three of us were equal partners and now I'm the only one left, so go for it. Look at whatever you want. I can tell you that the guys were excited about the possibilities based on panning results in the stream and the surface geology. They found some fairly large nuggets, which could indicate that the mother lode is nearby. Like most prospectors, they were looking for the hard rock origin of the stream gold. I'm guessing that most of their time out there was spent hiking in the rugged terrain of the stream headwaters, looking for some kind of surface indication of gold-bearing rock. I received one call from them about a week ago. They were happy, and it sounded like their surface explorations were indicative of extensive base metal mineralization. In other words, it looked good for finding gold, silver, and other stuff."

"What do you think would have been their next step?"

"Well, you can only tell so much from looking at rocks on the surface. The next step would probably have been core drilling to sample the rock layers and map the mineralization. But drilling in remote areas requires government permits, helicopter access, and expensive equipment, not to mention a much larger, centrally located camp. They would've needed some investors to help pay for it. So, I guess the actual next step would have been to convince potential partners of the value of the property."

Kate paged through the files. Notes in waterproof field books were mostly geological gobbledygook that she did not understand. Some of the cryptic notes seemed to suggest subdued excitement. There were photos of gold nuggets found in the stream with notations regarding the rough edges and lack of wear. Kate assumed the angular nuggets suggested the gold chunks had not traveled far enough to become smoothed by stream erosion processes, another indication that the mother lode might not be far away. She made copies of claim maps and aerial photos showing the boundaries of the SPG claim as well as the adjoining Northwest Base Metals claims to help guide any further investigations of the claim property. The neighboring claim area was large, consisting of several square miles – probably the result of combining a number of smaller claims. Nothing else in the files seemed important enough to be a motive for murder.

†

The next morning Charlie, JB, and Trooper Bob boarded the trooper speed boat and took off for the crime scene. Kate wanted to come along, but she had to work at her job as an administrative manager at FlashFrozen Seafood. She sometimes felt like she was the only one of the group that actually worked for a living and was pissed that work was interfering with life once again. Charlie's ecotour business was erratic, leaving lots of downtime, and JB did not do much of anything, although he claimed he was writing a scholarly treatise on contemporary politics.

The tough little boat pulled up to the shore at Jeremy and Jason's camp site. The trio disembarked and cautiously moved into the camp area. Bob and JB carried shotguns for bear protection, but there did not appear to be any additional bear sign. Apparently the bear had left now that the human carrion supply was gone. The day was sunny with light wind – all in all, a nice day for a hike in spite of the depressing recent history of the area. They walked single file along the creek up to the base of the mountainside where they had hiked before, then continued following the rough trail pioneered by the geologists, paralleling the cascading stream course. In some places they had to walk in the stream to avoid outcrops and large boulders. Fresh scars were seen on some of the exposed bedrock faces where the geologists had presumably chipped away at the rock to look at the minerology. After a half mile of difficult upslope hiking, the trio entered a sort of plateau that was devoid of trees. From there the trail took off to the west through dry, rocky terrain with no trees and scattered low-growing shrubs.

Charlie removed a set of maps from his pack and the group gathered around to get oriented. With the help of a portable GPS they determined that they were close to the western boundary of the claim that abutted the Northwest Base Metals claim. The boundary conveniently followed a line of longitude which made it easy to follow, and it was apparent that the geologists had frequently trekked the same route. They gained altitude rapidly as they climbed the steep slope characterized by a series of terrace-like steps separated by nearly impassable escarpments. As they neared the northwest corner of the claim property, they noted an area where the alders had been removed or trimmed to less than three feet high. Approaching more closely, they saw that a level platform had been constructed of cut logs, and portions of a one hundred square foot area had been trampled and were covered with exposed sandy dirt.

"Someone was core drilling here. A portable drill rig and personnel were brought in by helicopter, hence the landing pad. The light dirt is the result of drill cuttings and drill lubricating mud brought to the surface. You can see the hole over here," said Charlie. "I worked at a mine exploration camp years ago and have seen many of these core sites."

"If I'm not mistaken, this site is on Jeremy and Jason's claim property, which is mysterious since Janine said they haven't done any drilling yet. It looks like the property boundary is about three hundred feet west of here," remarked JB as he looked at their GPS position.

"OK, I guess we can assume that the neighboring miners were trespassing. They must have wanted the information badly to take such a chance. Judging from the trail up here it looks like our boys found this little incursion on their claim. We may be getting closer to finding a motive for their murders," said Bob.

"The only reason the company next door would drill here would be to fill in an important gap in the information that they already have," Charlie commented with a frown. "They use computer programs that take the information from the drill logs and construct a three-dimensional picture of the underground geology. The valuable ore must extend onto the SPG claim – maybe the most valuable ore."

"But, Charlie, wouldn't it make sense for Northwest Metals to try and form a partnership with SPG? They've already invested a lot of money and resources into exploration so it could be a good deal for both companies to join forces," added Bob.

"I'm guessing that greed is playing a part in all this. My cynical nature suggests that the folks at Northwest Metals want it all. Another aspect to all this is that the Northwest claim is landlocked, whereas

Jeremy and Jason's claim abuts saltwater, providing the potential for a port. That could be a very big deal in the ultimate development cost," said JB.

The super trooper was gazing out over the valley below them. "We may be getting ahead of ourselves. It's possible that the people next door simply made a mistake. Anyway, we obviously need to investigate further. It seems like a trip to the Northwest Metals camp may be a good place to start."

Chapter Four

The flute-like sounds of the Swainson's thrush seemed to come from all directions. These seldom seen but noisy birds sing continuously during the long daylight hours of Alaskan summers, providing one of the iconic sounds of northern forests. No man-made sounds interrupted the natural background of birds singing, insects buzzing, and squirrels scratching. Kate and Charlie sat on the small front porch of Kate's log cabin, which sat on high ground overlooking a black spruce bog. The slight breeze carried the scent of the bog and the sweet-smelling plants growing therein. It was late afternoon and they were taking a weekend break from dead bodies by relaxing, drinking beer, and talking about more trivial matters. Buster the cat was in his element, reveling in his newfound freedom and chasing dim-witted voles on the forest floor. He was clearly fed up with being confined to Charlie's boat cabin.

The small, one-room cabin was located west of Homer on a lonely road and accessed by a quarter-mile trail from a grassy parking area. The interior of the well-built structure was utilitarian with a home-built kitchen counter at one end, wood stove constructed of an oil barrel in the middle, a log slab table on one side, and a plywood bed on the other side. The kitchen sink consisted of a fiberglass utility sink that Kate had scrounged from the dump. The sink drain went through a hole in the floor, suggesting a somewhat questionable final destination. The minimalist fur-trapper décor was enhanced by various quirky additions provided by Kate's artistic flair. A mobile featuring abstract salmon hung from the rafters, and various curios and stuffed animals populated the many niches in the log walls. A very large stuffed purple hippo sat on the king-sized bed on top of a fluffy comforter. A worn but colorful Persian rug covered the floor in the center of the cabin.

Kate had purchased the inexpensive cabin a few weeks after arriving in Homer with money inherited from her grandmother. Her few local acquaintances at the time thought she was crazy and placed bets on how long she would last. The contrast between her previous place of residence — New York City — and off-the-grid Alaska living could not have been greater. But she stuck it out and gradually became comfortable with totally alien skills such as splitting wood and hauling water. The first winter had been rough, but Kate got pleasure from the challenge and found that she liked the solitude and quiet of her little cabin.

Kate's personal history, while short, was dramatic. She was raised by conservative, middle-class parents in a tree-lined suburb of a Michigan city. Her dogmatically religious father was a kind but somewhat difficult man. Following her family's plan for her future, she attended a Michigan state college. Much to her parents' dismay, she fell in with an artsy crowd and was convinced by an instructor that she had talent for dancing. Defying her parents, she dropped out of college in her junior year to pursue her dream in New York City. Unfortunately, the mean city did not cooperate. Several dance auditions failed to produce employment, and her relationships with men seemed always to lead to disappointment or worse.

The final straw occurred when her latest boyfriend punched her in the face while drunk. After he passed out, she gathered her meager possessions, piled them into her subcompact car, and started driving with no destination in mind.

Looking back on the day she left the city, Kate realized that she had had a breakdown of sorts. Much of the memory of driving across the U.S. and Canada was vague. One summer day she literally came to the end of the road in Homer without really knowing how she got there. This quirky Alaskan town bore no resemblance to anywhere she had ever been before, either culturally or ecologically. Having been populated by many vagabonds, misfits, and refugees from the 1960's, Homer was welcoming to strangers, and Kate arbitrarily decided to stay awhile.

After several seasonal jobs, Kate began working for FlashFrozen Seafood as an office gofer. Because of her intelligence and computer skills, she was soon able to snag a position as administrative manager. She had learned her computer skills from her older brother, James, who had been a serious hacker in high school and college. After a couple run-ins with the law, he had ostensibly reformed and now worked in the legitimate IT industry. Over the last few months Kate had sought to capitalize and improve on these skills by taking an online course in advanced information technology and coding. At the same time, she had been video conferencing with her brother, who was tutoring Kate in some of the finer points of illegal hacking, including some of his special tricks for avoiding detection while accessing forbidden networks.

Kate and Charlie had been brought together soon after Kate's arrival in Homer by dead bodies − one on the trail to her cabin and one floating next to Charlie's boat. Suddenly caught up in the same conspiracy, she and Charlie became friends and eventually lovers. Charlie had become smitten with Kate's daring nature, brains, and unconventional beauty. She had a lithe dancer's body, very long brown hair, Mediterranean complexion, and amazing big green eyes that somehow sucked him in to her soul. Her face was exotic, combining elements of eastern European and Irish ancestry.

The couple currently split their time between Kate's cabin and Charlie's boat. Since FlashFrozen was located next to the boat harbor, the Shearwater was obviously much more convenient, especially in the winter. But the cabin in the woods offered solitude and a peaceful vibe in spite of the fact that a wacko had tried to burn down the cabin two years earlier with them locked inside. Charlie's quick thinking had saved their lives and the cabin. Buster had awakened them and, thus, became a feline hero.

"This is really nice," Kate said while reclined on the slightly broken patio lounger, another item scavenged from the Homer dump. "It's too bad that we have to head back this afternoon to meet your flock of birdwatchers." Charlie was scheduled to lead a tour the next day.

"Mmm," grunted Charlie as he put down his book. "By the way, how is the computer stuff going?"

"I think I'm starting to get a feel for navigating the information world."

"So, what are you going to do with these new skills?" asked Charlie.

"I don't know. In the short term it may entitle me to a promotion at FlashFrozen. In the longer term I suppose I could do some IT consulting. But opportunities are sort of limited in Homer. Actually, I may be able to use some of these skills to help with our current crime-solving dilemma. There seem to be plenty of unknowns."

"It might be a good idea to look into the mysterious corporate structure of Northwest Base Metals if you can do it without getting arrested. I would miss you if you were in jail."

"You sure know how to sweet talk a woman," quipped Kate. "What happened to our agreement to not talk about dead bodies and current events?"

"Oops. On another topic, have you heard anything from your

parents lately?"

"I've had a couple of cordial emails from my mom. She said Dad is starting to accept that his daughter is living a life somewhat different from what he imagined. I also talked to my brother on the phone yesterday. He said that they are even talking about a trip to Alaska, which is a very scary prospect. I can't imagine what he will think after seeing our two alternative abodes, not to mention that I am living in sin with a boat bum."

"I'm not sure I agree with the 'bum' part, but we are definitely living in sin."

"You are a big help."

"If it makes you feel any better, I will be on my best behavior," said Charlie as he picked up his book. He was reading a biography of Benjamin Franklin. "Speaking of living in sin, old Ben was quite the ladies' man. He was mingling with the aristocracy of Paris and chasing young women while his wife was stuck alone in Philadelphia for years on end. Doesn't seem quite fair."

"It seems like a lot of history's ambitious men were womanizers, not to mention today's politicians. I guess it goes along with having power or prestige. Or maybe all men are just jerks."

"Some of my former girlfriends would probably agree with you. But in my case I'm just misunderstood."

"Yeah. Right," said Kate as she got up and sat on Charlie's lap.

"How's a guy supposed to read when he's being harassed?"

"Shut up. We have just enough time for an afternoon delight before we head back to town," replied Kate as she led Charlie into the cabin.

Chapter Five

The stupid outhouse is too far from the cabin, thought Bryce Cameron as he more or less ran down the path with a waddling gate, making it just in time. Bryce had been having gastrointestinal issues for the last several days. He knew he should probably go to the doctor, but that would entail flying his float plane from Lake Clark to Anchorage. He really was not feeling up to it. What if he had to poop during the flight? Although he owned a home in the city, it was currently occupied by his soon-to-be-ex-wife, and it was unlikely that she would welcome him under the current circumstances. Not to put too fine a point on it, but she hated his guts. Although his lifestyle suggested affluence — airplane, vacation home, city home, fishing boats — his actual financial situation was dismal. His marginal resources precluded staying in a hotel for any length of time, so his only option was the log cabin on the lakeshore within Lake Clark National Park. His family had owned the property for three generations; consequently, the private inholding was grandfathered within the park boundary. At least it was summer, and he did not have to feed the fireplace continually.

As he sat on the toilet, which consisted of a board with an oval hole in it, he thought about his disastrous investment in the Northwest Base Metals mine project located just twenty miles as the crow flies from his current location. The year's exploration work had proceeded smoothly except for the small detail that the mineral deposits were crap. It was possible that he would lose his entire investment — essentially his life savings. At the last briefing, the engineers told him that the best mineralization that included gold and silver was at the extreme northeast corner of the claim. It was likely that most of the potentially valuable ore was located on the neighboring claim. Although Bryce was the largest investor aside from the company executives, he had little actual input to company operations, which were based in Vancouver. He was frustrated that the company seemed unwilling to negotiate with the owners of the neighboring claim in any sort of cooperative way to develop what might be a very valuable resource. They were greedy and suspicious of Alaskans and had no patience for inconvenient Alaskan environmental regulations.

Bryce had intended that the mine development would be his final investment in preparation for retirement, but things were not working out the way he had planned. His instincts regarding investment potential had served him well until now. Now, however, he was beginning to realize that the NBM folks talked a good game but were basically full of shit. That asshole Gottlieb implied that once the mineral reserves were proved up, they would be able to sell the rights to a major mining company for big bucks, thus insuring that Bryce would be able to retire permanently to someplace warm. His impending divorce in combination with the poor exploration results caused a sudden reversal of his financial future. He couldn't believe that he had gone from one of Alaska's wealthiest persons to nearly bankrupt in only a few months. It was essential that the mine project succeed somehow, but he was not in control and had little recourse.

He waddled back to the cabin, lay down on the plush leather couch, and pulled a blanket up to his shoulders. Not only was he broke, but he felt really lousy.

Chapter Six

Charlie awoke early on Monday and devoted the next two hours to putting the Shearwater into shipshape condition for his guests, who were arriving on the ten o'clock plane from Anchorage. The forty-foot Shearwater had been originally designed as an Alaskan purse seine vessel, configured with a large back deck to store the long net, a hold in the middle of the boat to contain tons of flopping salmon, and a cabin/wheelhouse located well forward. Superstructure consisted of a mast, long boom, and a hydraulic power block used to haul the net. When used for fishing, the net was pulled off the back of the boat by a powerful skiff, creating a wall of net up to one thousand feet long designed to intercept or surround a school of salmon. The skiff stretched the net out and around the fish, making a complete circle back to the boat. As the net was reeled back in, the weighted line at the bottom of the net was pursed like a drawstring bag, and the fish caught in the bag were lifted into the boat.

But to accommodate Charlie's tourist business and live-aboard requirements, the Shearwater had been modified so that the deck became an observation area, the hold became a sleeping cabin, and the main cabin was spruced up to be more comfortable and inviting for guests.

Charlie swabbed the deck, cleaned the galley, stocked the refrigerator with drinks, and checked the engine's vital signs. Kate was forced to work around him as she ate breakfast and got ready for work. Buster had seen it all before and made himself scarce. After completing his chores, Charlie trudged up the harbor ramp to his old

SUV and proceeded to the Homer International Airport.

It always amused Charlie how easy it was to identify his wildlife tour clients from run-of-the-mill Alaskans as the passengers disembarked from the small commuter planes onto the tarmac. Almost without exception, their Eddie Bauer khaki outdoor clothes were crisp and clean, and their fleece jackets were from Patagonia. Often they had binoculars and cameras hanging from their necks. In contrast, most of the Alaska passengers could care less about the cleanliness or fashion appropriateness of their apparel. It was not necessary for Charlie to hold up a sign, as seen in most tourist destinations. He immediately recognized Jon and Sonia Mower and greeted them as they entered the terminal. Having shifted into his Alaska tour guide persona, he introduced himself, grabbed their duffel bags from the luggage return, and escorted them to his car.

He always tried to get some feel for his clients on the drive to the harbor by asking about their interests and home life. Some clients were sincerely interested in learning about stuff, and others just wanted to log experiences so they could brag to their friends back home. Some treated Charlie like a servant and others became lasting friends. Some past clients had been single-mindedly focused on adding birds to their life lists with very little actual interest in the ecological context. It turned out that the Mowers were friendly, well informed about avian natural history and ecology, and excited by the prospect of seeing things that they had not experienced before. They were enthusiastic bird watchers but did not view birding as a cutthroat competition.

"Wait. Stop!" yelled Sonia as they approached the harbor. "There's an eagle up there. That is so cool."

A bald eagle was perched on top of one of the harbor lamp posts. Charlie pulled over and the couple got out of the car with their telephoto lens equipped cameras and started clicking away while the inscrutable eagle stared back with apparent boredom. Eagles were very common on the Homer Spit thanks to the presence of fish-processing waste and other human debris. Some have considered the birds a public nuisance. Nevertheless, the birds were a significant tourist attraction, and Charlie had performed this routine with several other clients.

After parking in the lot above the harbor, Charlie led his clients to the ramp leading to the docks. "Why is the ramp so steep?" asked Sonia.

"The floating docks rise and fall with the tide, which can fluctuate as much as twenty-six feet. So, at extreme high tide the ramps are almost horizontal and at low tide, like right now, the ramps become hazardously steep," answered Charlie.

The party of three slid down the ramp while holding on to the railing and walked to the Shearwater. "So, why does Homer exist?" asked Sonia. Charlie began to realize that Sonia's curiosity was going to make the day interesting.

"Homer is a young community. Coal is one reason for early interest in the area. Exposed coal seams were observed by early mariners along the eroding bluffs – we'll be able to see some when we get out on the water. During the period 1895 to about 1910 the coal was mined in order to supply fuel to steamships plying Cook Inlet. But that quickly ended with the settlement of Anchorage and the discovery of other coal deposits to the north. For a while the Homer area languished and the town of Seldovia, across the bay, served as the gateway to Cook Inlet. During the pre-war period a few homesteaders and fishermen settled on the bench above the bay in what is now present-day Homer, but most of the activity was centered on the south side of Kachemak Bay. Herring fisheries and fox farming provided some short-lived economic success.

"In 1950 a road was constructed connecting Homer with Anchorage and the rest of the Alaska highway system. The highway connection between the towns was a significant engineering accomplishment because of the difficult terrain. After completion of the road, Homer became the primary supply hub for the southwestern Kenai Peninsula. The town has been growing ever since. Homer's natural beauty and abundant marine resources have attracted a wide variety of folks. Homer's out-of-the-way location has probably shaped its settlement demographics to a substantial degree. The area became a focal point for hippies and counterculture types in the 1960s and 1970s, many of whom are still here. Another interesting demographic is the presence of several communities of Russian Old Believers, a fundamentalist offshoot of the Russian Orthodox Church resulting from a schism dating back to the 1600s. Persecution over the years and especially after the Russian Revolution caused groups of Old Believers to leave Russia and disperse around the world. The Old Believer communities are insular and stubbornly maintain old traditions of dress and family structure. Commercial fishing has become an economic mainstay for the Alaska colonies.

"Once we get out onto the bay, I'll stop and answer any other questions on the ecology and geography of the area."

They loaded gear onto the boat and idled out of the harbor. Jon and Sonia were fascinated by the variety of boats in the harbor. Their cameras clicked as they observed big and small commercial fishing boats, sport-fish charter boats, private fishing boats, gleaming white fiberglass yachts, sail boats, and various indescribable derelict vessels. The boats were all mixed together, suggesting a somewhat more egalitarian approach to boat ownership than seen in most lower forty-eight harbors, where boats of various kinds are often segregated in an unstated caste system.

The Shearwater chugged south across the bay to Gull Island where Charlie's clients observed the thousands of cliff-nesting sea birds – kittiwakes, murres, puffins, and cormorants flew all around them, occasionally diving into the water or alighting on the cliffs. The scene was chaotic with birds in the sky, in the water, and on the cliff sides. As they got close to the cliffs, puffins could be seen underwater pursuing small fish using their wings for propulsion – essentially flying underwater. Several eagles soared overhead hoping to score a dead fish or a dead bird. The cameras were clicking so fast that Charlie almost expected the Nikons to start smoking. The Mowers were in ecstasy.

As his guests clicked away, the wind shifted and the putrid smell of bird guano wafted over the boat from the nesting cliffs. The smell brought Charlie back to the ill-fated camp of the geologists. Charlie could not help but think about dead, mutilated bodies. The vision of Jeremy Franks, or what was left of him, lying in the bushes was seared into his brain and would not go away. The whole thing was bizarre. What would motivate someone to travel to a remote site and kill two young men? The geologists were not a threat to anybody, at least not on the surface. Charlie was then brought back to earth by another of Sonia's questions.

"Is this incredible place protected?" asked Sonia.

"Gull Island is currently owned by the Seldovia Native Corporation and no one is permitted onshore. All of Kachemak Bay is considered a Critical Habitat Area, providing further protection. Gull Island has been the site of numerous seabird studies over the years because of its easy accessibility. The island is one of the largest kittiwake nesting areas in the world."

After the novelty of Gull Island had worn off, Charlie motored west to near Yukon Island and shut off the engine. A raft of sea otters hung on to kelp fronds and provided more photo ops. Otters would periodically peel off from the group, dive to the sea bottom, and resurface with an edible delicacy. Cracking sounds were heard as the furry critters used rocks to split open the shells of crabs or urchins. While Jon and Sonia watched the charismatic otters, Charlie continued his lecture on the Kachemak Bay natural setting.

"So, why does so much stuff live out here?" asked Sonia.

"A bunch of factors come together to make the marine environment unusually productive," answered Charlie. "Nutrient-rich water upwells from deep areas of the Gulf of Alaska and finds its way into Cook Inlet. Plus, many rivers contribute organic material and more nutrients from glacial erosion. Salmon streams not only contribute live fish to the fishery but also nutrients from salmon carcasses. The extreme tides enhance this dynamic, creating circular currents called gyres that concentrate nutrients and detritus. The resulting rich shellfish beds also attract fish. Halibut fishermen are well aware of the locations of gyres and local current conditions. Originally, Kachemak Bay supported huge runs of herring, but unfortunately the herring were badly depleted in the early twentieth century and haven't recovered. Other fisheries have seen fluctuations over the years, but commercial and sport fishing remain one of the area's most important economic drivers."

The Shearwater continued its journey, threading its way through the islands on the south side of Kachemak Bay. Bird observations and camera clicking were more or less continuous, culminating in sightings of pigeon guillemots, which neither of the Mowers had seen before. The funny orange-legged diving birds were seen perched on tiny ledges on sheer cliffs, repeatedly lighting on the water below, diving for fish, and returning to their perches.

The intrepid tour group reached the small isolated town of Seldovia in time for a late lunch. Located in a very scenic spot on the edge of Seldovia Bay, the town had a cozy vibe and laid-back atmosphere. While eating lunch at a small café, Charlie explained, "Seldovia has had a much longer history than Homer. Sequential waves of native Alaskans representing both Athabaskan and southern Eskimo groups settled the Seldovia Bay area prehistorically, followed by Russian explorers and settlers in the latter part of the eighteenth century. The Russians notoriously enslaved native Aleuts and forced them to hunt sea otters. Seldovia reached its heyday in the early twentieth century fueled by herring fisheries, fur farming, and other commercial fisheries.

"One of the more interesting aspects of Seldovia's history has to do with the disastrous 1964 Good Friday earthquake. The town thought it had escaped most of the quake damage including the tsunamis that caused many fatalities in other coastal towns. But several weeks after the quake a high spring tide flooded portions of the town, rising above the level of boardwalks and storefronts supported on pilings at water's edge. At first, residents assumed the tides had gotten higher, but, after some studies, it was discovered that the whole town had subsided by a couple of feet. Large portions of the original seaside boardwalk were now below high tide levels and flooded several times a year. Federal disaster funds were used to reconfigure the waterfront on higher ground. Today Seldovia is a sleepy town of a few hundred people. Economic incentives are obviously limited."

"Wouldn't it be kind of inconvenient living here with no road connection?" asked Sonia.

"Yeah. But there are regular flights and ferries from Homer, and the people here enjoy their solitude."

"I think it's pretty nice," said Jon. "Let's move here."

"You might want to think that through," said Sonia. "You're pretty fond of suburban amenities."

"I don't know. This café has espresso. That's all I need," replied Jon.

Re-boarding the Shearwater, they headed back to Homer. During the fifteen-mile trip they were lucky enough to see a humpback whale, an infrequent Kachemak Bay visitor. Once back on terra firma Charlie gratefully accepted a check for the tour and dropped Jon and Sonia at their bed and breakfast. It had been a good day with another satisfied customer.

But Charlie kept thinking about other things.

Chapter Seven

The next morning, a Tuesday, Charlie awakened early and emerged from the below-deck master suite to take advantage of his favorite time of day. Buster the cat followed him up the companionway stairs and immediately went to his litterbox. Then with a satisfied look on his face, he draped himself over the pilot house roof, looking like feline roadkill. Kate was still snuggled below in the down sleeping bag and would be sleeping for another hour before she had to get up to go to work. Charlie gazed at the scenery around him. The glaciers across Kachemak Bay glistened in the morning sunlight. The dramatic volcanic peaks across Cook Inlet stood out in brilliant profile like triplicate Fujis. The Kenai Mountains on the south side of the bay began to take on the pinkish-purple pastels of sunrise alpenglow. Within the Homer Harbor basin, the dewy rigging of the boats created a spider's web of reflected light. The weather was warm and the wind was calm. The intensely organic smell of the mud flats exposed by the low tide filled his nostrils. Many would find the smell unpleasant, but Charlie found it comforting – like the horse lover who yearns for the smell of stables.

His thoughts went back to when he had first arrived in Homer and all the weird stuff that had happened since he had limped into town in the mid-1990s in his ancient Chevy pickup. Originally from coastal New England, he grew up in a loving family. His father was an engineer and his mother was a musician. His dad had always encouraged him to do whatever felt right. Since childhood he had been entranced by the romance of the sea and the mystique of coastal communities. After graduating from a state college with a biology degree, he roamed around looking for a suitable place to pursue his passion for commercial fishing. Since the New England fisheries were pretty much shot, he naturally found his way to Alaska. Finding himself at the end of the road with dwindling funds and a truck that was about to die, he had little choice but to pause in his search. Fortunately, he fell in love with Homer which combined spectacular scenery, coastal ambience, and the wildness of the Last Frontier. Working as a deckhand on various commercial fisheries, he earned the respect of the fishermen because of his endurance and biological savvy. Charlie saved his money and blew it all on the Shearwater in order to pursue his dream of providing seafood for the masses. However, a combination of low fish numbers and poor market prices forced him to rethink his career plans. He spent most of a year refitting his boat for the tourist trade, and, at the same time, he converted the utilitarian fishing boat into a comfortable live-aboard.

Currently, Charlie was living quite comfortably, guiding wildlife cruises in Kachemak Bay, supplemented with whatever work he could find in the off season. Charlie had gradually come to be regarded as an "Alaska character," a persona he cultivated to enhance his appeal to out-of-state tourists. His full blonde beard, shaggy blonde hair, bright blue eyes, broad shoulders, and six-foot-plus height worked together to give him a sort of Viking-like appearance that especially appealed to persons of the opposite sex. A Greek fisherman's cap topped off his salty persona.

Charlie's history of female companionship was somewhat checkered. He had been involved in several relationships that had ended badly. He had the reputation of being averse to commitment, especially if it involved changing his lifestyle. His girlfriends had not been enthusiastic about spending their lives on a boat with someone whose annual income was highly unpredictable. However, his outlook was changing, and his current partner, Kate, had taken things to a new level. He was remarkably content. The fact that they had met over dead bodies two years before seemed to have somehow made them more intimate.

His time in Homer had been punctuated by a couple of forays into investigations of mysterious local happenings that had interrupted his life in various ways. It seemed like he just had a way of stumbling onto situations involving unsavory characters. In the most recent episode, Charlie, Kate, and JB had worked with local law enforcement and the Drug Enforcement Agency to end a complex drug distribution syndicate that had roots in Homer. In the process they had become targeted themselves.

The odd trio of Charlie, Kate, and JB were bonded by their past adventure, mutual curiosity, and desire to make things right. One of the surly players involved in their past entanglements had sarcastically called them the three mooseketeers. The silly name had stuck.

Chapter Eight

Early on Wednesday morning, Bob the Super Trooper sat in his tiny office at his gray metal Army surplus desk, opened an email from Dr. Mort, and saw that the pathologist had attached a preliminary autopsy report. He sat back in his rickety desk chair and scanned the four pages of information. No big surprises – both men had been killed by gunshot wounds. The hole in Jeremy's skull was, of course, pretty obvious. But Jason's wound was less apparent. Because of bear munching and decomposition, an entry wound to the chest had not been superficially visible, but dissection had clearly shown that a bullet tracked through ribs, into the heart, and lodged against the spine. The bullet was a 9 mm and appeared to be in good enough shape for a ballistics match. Whoever had killed them was a very good shot, targeting lethal areas.

At nine-thirty Bob drove to the Homer Airport where he had reserved a helicopter to take him to the Northwest Base Metals exploration camp. Charlie and JB showed up a few minutes later. All three climbed into the Jet Ranger and strapped in. Mike, the pilot and owner of Kachemak Choppers, was an aging Vietnam vet who had spent so many hours in helicopters that all operations were purely instinctual. While nearing age seventy, Mike's eyesight and coordination were still sharp, and Bob would not fly with anyone else.

As the helicopter climbed and turned to the west, the spectacular view of Lower Cook Inlet and its volcanic peaks came into view. At ninety miles per hour it took only twenty minutes to cross the gray water of the inlet to the opposite shore. The machine climbed over a piedmont-like area and into the rugged Aleutian Range. Mike had been to the mining camp before on supply runs and flew directly to the site. The NBM camp was located in a pretty valley. Small stream courses descended the valley sides contributing to a larger stream that flowed south along the valley floor. The camp structures were located on a low terrace just above the stream. All in all, it was a very pleasant location.

During their descent, another helicopter, a bright blue Hughes 500 machine, could be seen across a meadow in the process of lifting a sling net loaded with timbers at the end of a long cable, presumably heading to a drill site somewhere on the property. These small but powerful machines were often preferred at remote work sites because of their maneuverability and ability to get in and out of small spaces, as well as their ability to lift heavy loads.

The camp was typical of remote facilities throughout Alaska, consisting of portable structures made of heavy vinyl stretched over steel hoops to form Quonset-like structures. Often insulation was sandwiched between two layers of vinyl. Charlie recalled sleeping in one of the structures during a rain storm – when the rain hit the tightly stretched fabric it was like being inside a drum.

As the group from Homer landed, several people emerged from the largest of the Quonset huts, presumably an operations center. The first man to approach was tall and swarthy with the build of a linebacker. He had a semiautomatic handgun in a holster on his hip. Openly carried guns were not illegal or unusual in the Alaska wilderness, but Bob thought it was a little odd that he would be wearing it around camp. Bob's trooper uniform seemed to cause a change of attitude among the approaching group from somewhat hostile to welcoming. A subtle nod from the oldest of the men signaled the linebacker to back off.

Bob concluded that the guy was some kind of security person.

"Good morning," Bob said. "Have you guys got a few minutes to talk?"

"Sure. Let's go into the office. I'm Craig Johnson, chief mining engineer, and my young associate is Joel Spurgeon, our geologist."

The three visitors introduced themselves and shook hands. The linebacker was not introduced. All six men entered the hut and sat at a small conference table. Scattered around the space were desks, drafting tables, and long narrow boxes containing rock core samples. A woman was pounding away at a computer at the far end.

"So, what's this all about?" asked Craig.

"I'm guessing you guys are aware that preliminary exploration has been going on at the claim next to yours to the east," replied Bob. "One of your drill sites was clearly located on their claim, so there are probably some trespass issues."

"Wow," replied Craig. "I didn't know that anyone was working over there, and I definitely didn't know that our drill program was on their claim. If that's true, then somebody fucked up. I'm sure we can work something out with our neighbors so that there will be no need to pursue things further."

"That would be great," Bob said, "except that the two principals of South Peninsula Gold were murdered at their camp sometime last week." Charlie and JB tried to get some feeling for the reaction of the three men at the table by carefully watching their eyes. The two miners were either genuinely surprised, or they were exceptional actors. Linebacker's face was a cold mask that hid any reaction.

"That's horrible," Craig replied. "I can understand why you felt compelled to come up here and question us, but we didn't have anything to do with it."

"OK," sighed Bob. "Obviously, the investigation is still in its early stages and we're looking at all options. Can you folks account for your whereabouts for the last ten days or so?"

"I think all of us in here have constantly been in camp during that time period," Craig said. "I guess we can alibi each other."

"I took a helicopter into Homer last Thursday to pick up a part," said Joel Spurgeon. "But I came right back. The pilot can verify that."

"What other employees are currently in camp?" asked Bob.

"The drillers and chopper pilot are out at work sites. The chopper mechanic is sleeping since he works at night. The cook and her helper are in the mess hall. I can ask them to come here if you want," said Craig.

"It would be better if we went to them, if that's all right with you," replied Bob. "Just a few more questions. A guy representing your company named Hank Gottfried stopped at the South Peninsula Gold office some time ago and inquired whether they would be willing to sell their claim rights. They respectfully declined since their exploration efforts had just gotten underway. Gottfried seemed quite upset that they weren't cooperating. I understand he is from your home office in Vancouver. Do you have a contact phone number for him?"

"Yeah. Darlene, can you get Gottfried's number for us?"

"So, how is your project going so far? Any luck?" asked JB

"The results of our core sampling are proprietary, but we are optimistic that the property has some value," replied Craig.

"One more question – can you give us the name of your colleague at the end of the table?" Bob asked.

Linebacker finally spoke. "What do you need that for?"

"It's standard procedure in an investigation to get everyone's name," replied Bob.

"His name is Max Karelian," said Craig.

"What is Mr. Karelian's role on your project?" asked Bob.

"He is our head of security."

"Why do you feel you need an armed security man at an isolated exploration camp?" asked JB.

"The competition between companies looking for good opportunities is fierce, and our fellow gold prospectors tend to be a jealous and sneaky bunch. Plus, we have had various bears hanging around camp," Craig replied.

"It's probably worth noting that a 9 mm handgun is not the optimum bear protection weapon," Bob remarked as he rose from the table. His eyes glanced over Max's gun before turning back to Craig. "Anyway, thanks for your time. I'm sure you'll be hearing from us."

"Would it be possible to get a list of people currently in camp?" asked Charlie as he and JB stood to leave.

Craig started to answer, but Max cut him off and said, "Personnel records are confidential. Without a warrant we don't have to comply."

"That's true," replied Bob. "We were hoping for your voluntary cooperation."

As they went out the door, Charlie turned toward Craig and said, "You might think about providing the results of your illicit core sample to what's left of South Peninsula Gold. I imagine the information could be valuable when they go to sell the claim."

The informal investigative team wandered over to the mess hall. The cook, Marlene Frye, was a large fifty-something-year-old woman with braided blond hair and a somewhat mannish appearance. Her bright blue eyes had an alertness that suggested intelligence. Her assistant and camp housekeeper, Betty, was a shy, petite young woman in her late teens. Both were working in the kitchen and looked surprised when they saw Bob in his trooper uniform.

"What's up?" Marlene said as they approached.

"We're investigating some bad stuff that happened on the claim east of here. Do you have time to answer some questions?" asked Bob.

"Sure. Fire away."

"Have you guys been in camp for the last ten days or so?"

"Yep. We're committed for a two-month stretch."

"Have you seen any of the other camp personnel leave the claim area?"

"With the camp chopper buzzing around all day it's hard to tell where they are all the time. But they've all been around for breakfast and dinner. Can I ask exactly what it is that you're investigating?"

"Two geologists exploring the claim next door were murdered in their camp by the inlet."

"Holy shit! And you think someone from here might be involved?"

"We don't know. We're just asking questions at this stage," replied Bob. "Have you noticed anyone acting strange or suspicious?"

"No, not really. The security guy, Max, is creepy as hell, but he mostly keeps to himself. Nobody can really understand what he is doing here."

"Do any of the drillers stand out for any reason?" asked Charlie.

"Well, they're all rude, sexist, and obnoxious. But, other than that, nothing out of the ordinary. One guy named Travis seems to sometimes keep to himself. He usually eats after the crowd has left," said Marlene.

"Do you know Travis' last name?" asked Bob.

"No. The personnel records are all kept in the office. I guess that's sort of unusual. In camps like this, the cooks often have responsibility for billeting."

"OK, thanks. We'll let you get back to it. I'm going to give you one of my cards. If you see or hear anything that might be of interest, give me a call if you can. Meanwhile, be careful. If anyone asks you what we talked about, just tell them we asked about your alibis for the last week and to confirm that the honchos were here the whole time," said Bob.

As Bob, Charlie, and JB walked back across the length of the camp area,

JB memorized as many details about the camp as he could without being too conspicuous. He noticed that there was a small, sturdy metal building near the trees at the edge of the cleared area. The building seemed out of place since all the other structures were designed to be portable and temporary.

In the chopper, on the way back to Homer, Bob asked for initial impressions of the meeting with the mine officials. All the passengers had head phones to block the engine noise and provide a connection to the helicopter's intercom system.

"I think Craig was lying about the trespass issues but not about the murders. It's hard to know what Karelian's role may be. I've never known a small remote operation like that to have a security staff. Sometimes there are dedicated bear guards, but they are usually locals armed with shotguns. Anyway, Max's presence is a red flag," Charlie said.

"I agree with Charlie's assessment. Max had the look of a former military guy, so his skills probably lie in the realm of defense against intruding human beings rather than Alaskan wildlife. There is something going on with those guys, but I have no idea how it ties in with the murders," JB replied.

Mike the chopper pilot had been listening in on the conversation. "I've made two prior trips to the mine camp to deliver parts for machinery. Both times I was instructed to remain in the helicopter while they inspected the delivery packages. Normally in situations like that the pilots are treated like royalty since they represent a connection to the outside world for the camp workers. Cultivating friendly relations leads to pilots doing favors – delivering mail, bringing newspapers, and maybe even a McDonald's hamburger. Their degree of paranoia is definitely unusual."

†

It was still early when Bob got back to the office so he ran names through law enforcement and other internet databases. Craig Johnson was a Canadian citizen with no U.S. criminal record and nothing egregious from Canada. Joel Spurgeon was an American from Fairbanks and had a clean record. Max Karelian was a little more interesting. He apparently had enlisted in the U.S. Army at age eighteen and graduated from Special Forces school followed by two tours in Afghanistan. After an honorable discharge he had been involved in a couple of minor assaults, probably bar fights, but nothing significant. He was then employed by a defense contractor as a sort of mercenary and had spent a couple more years in Afghanistan. The contractor, Unified Defense Systems (UDS), had been accused of mistreatment of Afghani civilians and relieved of their duties. Karelian was named as one of the UDS employees involved in the scandal. The resulting lawsuit ended in a settlement agreement with none of the participants receiving jail time. Bob was unable to find any information on Gottfried other than a Vancouver address.

†

That evening Craig Johnson and Max Karelian sat by themselves at a table in the small camp mess hall. "So, Max, what's the deal with the murders. Do you have any idea?"

"No."

"OK. I'll call Gottfried in the morning and find out what he wants to do about the trespass situation and let him know about our neighbor's misfortune. But meanwhile, it's obvious that we are going to be prime suspects in the killings. We have a pretty strong motive, given that the best mineralization is on their claim. Gottfried's visit to South Peninsula Gold combined with the errant drill site provide a pretty strong indication that we need that property."

"I don't think we need to worry. There's no evidence connecting us to the murders, and we can probably work out some kind of information sharing with SPG so that the trespass thing appears as an advantage for them since they'll be getting some free information. The core records could probably be falsified in some way."

"Why did you refuse to give them an employee list?"

"It's none of their business."

Craig was not so sure that Max's cavalier attitude was reasonable. He considered himself a shrewd judge of character and, while the trooper might lack imagination, he was worried about Charlie and JB. He was not quite sure why the two civilians had accompanied the trooper, but he was pretty sure it meant trouble. Furthermore, Max's idea of falsifying the core records was naïve. Any lawyer would require some kind of verification process. It would probably be possible to switch the actual rock cores and relabel the boxes, but greater complexity meant more room for error. Plus, any future core drilling would contradict the false samples and possibly lead to legal trouble. He was getting more and more uneasy about the whole situation. He knew that Karelian was more than just a security person – he was originally hired by the home office and probably provided eyes and ears for the Vancouver guys.

Although nominally the field boss, Craig's role as mining engineer was primarily to map the mineral resources and determine their value and the engineering feasibility of mining. He was beginning to get very suspicious of the other NBM employees and their personal agendas. Max's refusal to hand over an employee list added more suspicion. Why would he care? He also wondered what role their Alaskan investor, Bryce Cameron, played in the overall scheme of things. His feeling was that Bryce was a patsy who had been courted by the Vancouver staff as a gullible source of money. But he did not know for sure what Bryce's motive was. Worst of all, he was not at all positive that Karelian had not murdered the guys next door. Aside from the obvious immorality, which he did not take lightly, he did not understand how such violence could advance development of a mine. Things were getting weirder and weirder. He began to think about somehow disentangling himself from the whole project.

Chapter Nine

Later that same evening, JB sat at his tiny desk in the cabin of the *Otterly Ridiculous*. Like most below-deck sailboat cabins, it was dark. Mahogany paneling and twelve-volt lighting contributed to the gloom. But JB liked it. It somehow fit his personality. Their visit that morning to the mine camp had seriously piqued his curiosity – something was definitely going on with those guys. He pulled a book on twentieth-century political movements from the little shelf above his desk, turned to page 121, and extracted a note with a long alphanumeric code. On his laptop he opened a web site that displayed only a Celtic design. Typing the code resulted in an encrypted email form. On the form he typed *"any info on a Canadian company called Northwest Base Metals Consortium?"*

He exited the site and opened the file for his current book project, which was currently on the second chapter. As usual, he sat and stared at the page – yet another day of writer's block. During his mental wanderings he began to contemplate how he had ended up in this odd community at the end of the road.

Johann Sebastian Bachman – known by everyone as JB – arrived in Homer a few years after Charlie. He had never been quite sure whether his parents had given him his name as a joke or whether they actually respected the original Johann Sebastian. One late summer day he limped into the harbor in his almost derelict thirty-five-foot sailboat. He set up housekeeping in the available slot next to Charlie's boat, and the sailboat had not moved from its spot ever since. As the years went by, the topside of the *Otterly Ridiculous* became more and more cluttered with the debris of living aboard. In earlier years, prior to the legalization of cannabis in Alaska, the water and fuel containers, ropes, and buoys were joined in the summer by a six-foot-tall marijuana plant. The plant achieved almost legendary status among the harbor community. When authorities finally cracked down, selected portions of the plant were consumed at a giant wake held on the beach for the departing flora.

JB's physical appearance was unusual. He was tall and lanky with a wild demeanor, resembling a cross between Ichabod Crane and a mad scientist. His brown hair was shoulder length, permanently disheveled, and usually sticking straight out as if suffering from permanent static cling. His dark brown eyes had a sort of wild, unsettling intensity. His clothing trended toward collegiate 1960s sloppy, complemented by his large collection of Grateful Dead T-shirts.

As boat neighbors, he and Charlie became friends. JB was one of the smartest people Charlie had ever met, and despite being quirky and often stoned on weed, he was able to analyze complex situations at a rapid rate. Because JB avoided talking about his past, Charlie had gotten curious and Googled his name, but information was sparse. The most prominent post was an editorial in a student newspaper from a southern California university, which indicated the student body was very upset that Professor Bachman was being fired because of an affair with one of his students. Apparently he was very popular with the students, and a major controversy erupted between students and faculty. Other posts indicated that he had received a PhD in political science in his late twenties. There were absolutely no records of JB's life before that time.

It had become apparent during the prior year when the gang was dealing with the drug syndicate that JB had special skills and government contacts, suggesting some kind of unusual intelligence experience. Finally, JB had divulged that he had left home at age seventeen and been intensively trained for intelligence work over the following eight or nine years. JB suggested to Charlie that he left the weird world of covert operations because he had come to believe that it was immoral. So, now he lived on his sailboat with no known source of income and was supposedly working on a scholarly book having to do with the roots of the divisive politics of the twenty-first century.

JB's phone rang, startling him and bringing him out of his reverie. He saw that it was an unlisted number and gladly answered it. "Good evening, Karl. Thanks for getting back to me."

"Johann, I haven't heard from you in a couple of years. What have you gotten involved in now?"

"More mysterious murders in the far north. Were you able to get any information on Northwest Base Metals?"

"A little bit. They're not exactly transparent. The complicated corporate structure with companies inside of companies appears designed to obfuscate. Some of the people involved are known to Canadian authorities and may have intriguing connections to Chinese attempts to infiltrate Canadian and American tech companies for purposes of industrial espionage and other anti-competitive mischief, but it's mostly a shadow company and nobody knows much about them. Why do you ask?"

"They're trying to develop a mine of some kind in Alaska. They may be responsible for killing two geologists on a neighboring claim, suggesting that they want the claim very badly."

"That seems kind of drastic. I wish I could provide more information, but I'll make some more inquiries. Meanwhile, be careful. One of my sources suggested the involvement of a triad crime gang possibly connected to the central government of China."

"Great. Thanks, Karl. I owe you another one."

"I probably won't collect on the debt. Take care," said Karl as he signed off. Karl had been JB's boss during a darker time in his life. Normally communications like what had just occurred would be forbidden, but JB and Karl had a special affection for each other. Additionally, JB knew where numerous figurative bodies – as well as literal ones –were buried. The information could seriously embarrass Karl and his old agency. So they had worked out a way to talk to each other.

Chapter Ten

The following morning Lee Chen walked briskly down Pender Street in Vancouver's Chinatown. Passing a butcher shop with various sad-looking deceased animals hanging from hooks in the display window, he entered a nondescript shabby doorway between shops, went up a narrow staircase, and entered a spacious second-floor office with windows overlooking the bustling traffic and pedestrians on the street below. While the street entrance had a squalid appearance, Lee Chen's office was clean, bright, and well furnished with oriental artwork and ancient artifacts. Large maps and aerial photos were displayed on one wall along with odd-looking vertical charts labeled with Mandarin characters. Wooden cases contained weighty books on geology, metallurgy, and chemistry. Some books were in English and others were in Mandarin. Lee's large, beautiful antique desk was made of age-darkened mahogany with ornate scroll work on the front and sides. On the desk were two computers, one using Mandarin characters and the other English letters. Lee was fully capable of fluently working on either one.

He began reviewing geological data sent to his English computer, translating the data into Chinese, and entering it into the other computer. The multicolored image on the screen displayed three-dimensional profiles of projected underground minerology based on sequential core samples. The rock strata between cores was estimated by projecting the core information forward, backward, and sideways — sort of like a connect-the-dots puzzle. The software allowed the images to be rotated in any direction providing various perspectives. Calculating the volume of selected formations was another important function. The computers, of course, did all the hard work.

It was time for his daily report to the home office in Beijing. He encrypted the image files and sent them off to his bosses. As he started to type the encrypted email that would describe progress on his secret project, his mobile phone rang. The caller ID said Hank Gottfried. Lee did not like to be interrupted and swore under his breath that Canadian businessmen have no patience.

"This is Lee Chen. What news do you have for me, Mr. Gottfried?"

"Our northern operation had a visit from the police. It seems two geologists working at the claim next door have been murdered. Also, they know that one of our drill sites was outside the claim boundary. First of all, how do you want us to handle the trespass issue? And second, do you know anything about the murders?"

"I don't know anything about people being killed. I think any further conversation on this topic should be in person." With that, Lee Chen hung up.

Mouthing several Chinese epithets, Lee sat back and began to wonder how his team could be so incompetent. He had no idea how he would explain these complications to Beijing. Lee had no moral compunction relative to disposing of people who got in the way of his plans, but this particular action only complicated things and did not advance his interests. He completed his email without mentioning the latest news from Alaska. Lee then texted a message to Hank Gottfried arranging a meeting the next day at a Chinatown restaurant to discuss the project.

†

It was a typical Saturday morning in the main cabin of the Shearwater. Charlie and Kate slept in, emerging mid-morning from their cozy stateroom in the former fish hold under the back deck of the utilitarian vessel. Charlie was especially proud of his master suite on the Shearwater. He had converted what had been a large empty space into a beautiful, teak-lined bedroom with a queen bed, built-in shelves and cabinets, and a tiny head with a shower. The woodwork followed the curvature of the hull and was all custom fitted. No off-the-shelf components from a big-box store were used in the process.

Charlie began the ritual of cooking bacon and eggs on the old brass-fronted Bristol stove while Kate sat drinking coffee and reading the Homer News. In the process of remodeling the boat Charlie had tried to retain as much of the workboat atmosphere as possible, including preservation of the original diesel stove. These stoves, which provide heat for both cooking and cabin warmth, are found in almost all Alaskan fishing boats. Often the stoves are left burning year-round to warm the cabin, minimize condensation, and prevent plumbing from freezing. A coffee pot can almost always be found sitting on the warm stove top.

Neither of the occupants were surprised when JB dramatically leaped on board by swinging from the rigging, his gangly body and long arms reminding Kate of an orangutan. He mysteriously always knew when food was imminent. JB's T-shirt du jour featured a portrait of Jerry Garcia in mid-concert with a caption that said, *"I'm not really dead."* He had a drawer full of Grateful Dead-themed shirts which allowed a rotation of about ten days before having to recycle T-shirts. As usual, his hair was standing on end, providing an Einstein vibe that may, or may not, have been intentional.

"Alright, who called this meeting?" JB said as he helped himself to coffee and sat next to Kate.

"Actually, no one. But since you're here, you might as well have some breakfast," replied Charlie.

"I thought you'd never ask."

"As it turns out Bob should be here in a few minutes. He wanted to talk about dead guys, so your arrival is timely," Charlie said.

As if on cue, the Shearwater suddenly listed to starboard and the Super Trooper clambered on board. Bob was a large man – not fat exactly – but tall and built like an old-growth tree stump. His size seemed incompatible with his roundish baby face and crew-cut hair.

"Hey, Bob. What's happening?" Kate greeted from over her coffee cup.

"I figured after the events of last year I might as well consult with you guys right away since you're going to poke your noses in to the deaths anyway."

JB was shoveling food into his mouth and said between bites, "Our superb crime fighting team is here to help where we can. So, where does the investigation stand?"

"There's not much new to report. I did manage to get one of our investigators to look into the public records for Northwest Metals. I guess it's a privately held company with just a few stockholders. One thing that might be interesting is that one of the named investors is an Alaskan with an Anchorage address named Bryce Cameron. I called the listed number and talked to his soon-to-be-ex-wife, who is not currently very fond of Mr. Cameron. She kicked him out of the house a few weeks ago, and she assumes he is currently living on family property within Lake Clark National Park. He has no phone and commutes by float plane when he needs to. I asked about the Northwest Metals project, and I could almost hear her rolling her eyes. She said it was a stupid investment and is part of the reason that she is so pissed. Apparently, he donated most of their life savings to the project. She asked what the inquiry was about so I told her we were in the early stages of collecting information relating to some bad things that happened on a neighboring claim. She then sounded concerned and said that Bryce, while sometimes not too smart, would never be involved with violence."

"Who are the other stockholders?" Charlie asked.

"Hank Gottfried and the mining engineer, Craig Johnson, own less than ten percent each. The largest share – fifty-one percent – is owned by a mysterious Canadian corporation called Salish Sea Ventures. It seems to be a holding company with no real business other than the Alaska mine. The actual ownership of Salish Sea is unknown."

"That's pretty interesting," JB said as he swallowed another mouthful of eggs. "As it happens, I did a bit of research on my own. There's not much known about the company itself, but apparently some of the people involved have connections with Chinese attempts to create havoc in North America, and, what is more ominous, there may be connections with Chinese organized crime. We really need to know what those guys are up to."

"I don't suppose it would do any good to ask where you got this information," said Bob.

"Probably not," answered JB.

Kate looked at Bob with concern. "If all this has international implications, shouldn't we get the FBI involved?"

"I can't really base a request for FBI backup only on JB's secret source. Let's see how things play out for a while," replied the Super Trooper.

"So, where do we go from here?" Kate asked.

"We should probably try to talk to this Bryce Cameron guy and see what he knows," Bob said. "The troopers have an as-needed floatplane contract with Churchill Air Service, so it wouldn't cost much to fly to

Lake Clark and pay Mr. Cameron a visit."

"I agree," Charlie said. "Another thing I'd like to do is go through the South Peninsula Gold files again and see if I can find anything interesting that might help unravel the puzzle."

"Beverly is going to be here next week. Maybe I can coerce her to use her DEA connections and business knowledge to ferret out secrets hiding behind the Salish Sea Corporate wall. But I don't want her to get in trouble with her boss," added JB.

"Well, OK. Looks like we have a plan," said Bob. "I'll set up a flight to Lake Clark for Monday morning. My bosses might not be too happy about civilians on a trooper charter. I may need a reason for you guys to participate."

"Isn't our total awesomeness enough?" said JB.

"Didn't that expression go out of style about twenty years ago?" Kate quipped.

"I'm sort of a retro kind of guy," mumbled JB through a mouthful of purloined scrambled eggs.

"Alright, I'll think of something," said Bob. "Meanwhile, who wants to go on a flightseeing trip?"

"I'll go," Charlie said. "I have a charter starting on Wednesday so Monday should be good."

"Me too," JB chimed in.

"I'd love to go," Kate said. "But, unlike you guys, I have to work."

Chapter Eleven

The Super Trooper and JB were waiting at the Churchill Air float plane dock on Beluga Lake when Charlie arrived. They piled into the de Havilland Beaver piloted by Frank Churchill. Frank was in his mid-fifties and had been doing the Alaska bush pilot thing for a long time. There was little wind and high overcast as they accelerated over the smooth surface of the lake, rose up over the trees, and headed southwest over Cook Inlet. The large radial engine of the old Beaver was incredibly loud, making conversation impossible. About two-thirds of the way across the inlet the plane passed along the side of Augustine Volcano, which sits atop uninhabited Augustine Island. The volcano is a perfect representation of the classic conical volcano shape. After about twenty minutes flying time the plane reached the west shore of the inlet, passed over a series of ridges separated by spruce forest, small lakes, and muskeg, then crossed the east end of Lake Iliamna, third largest lake completely within the U.S.

Besides being a nursery area for millions of juvenile salmon that will ultimately contribute to the huge Bristol Bay fishery, Lake Iliamna is home to the famed Iliamna monster. This ancient native legend of a mysterious creature in the lake has been somewhat corroborated in modern times by numerous supposed sightings of a large fish-like animal more than fifteen feet long. The lake contains one of the world's only populations of freshwater seals, and these animals have sometimes been suggested as the source of the legend. Alternatively, Beluga whales sometimes swim up the Kvichak River from Bristol

Bay and enter the lake to feed on salmon. But some of the more trustworthy observations suggest an elongated creature with a vertical tail like a fish rather than a horizontal tail like a marine mammal. Consequently, sturgeon and sharks have been suggested as possibly fitting the size and description. An Anchorage newspaper at one time offered a $100,000 reward for proof of the existence of Illie, the monster. But, like the Loch Ness monster, proof has been hard to come by.

After crossing Lake Iliamna, the Churchill Air Beaver followed the Newhalen River from where it enters Lake Iliamna to its outlet at the south end of Lake Clark. Sections of the river appeared dark red from the large, dense schools of sockeye salmon making their way upstream. Lake Clark is a long, narrow body of water that sits in a spectacular crack between mountains of the Aleutian Range about a hundred miles from Homer. It can be a dangerous place to fly in bad weather, but the visibility was good and they had no problems. The waters are a startling milky turquoise blue because of the presence of colloidal rock flour eroded from the many glaciers that contribute melt water to the lake.

Frank knew exactly where Cameron's cabin was located. The number of private residences within the national park is limited, and most inhabitants were well known among the floatplane fraternity. Descending toward a small inlet about midway on the west shore, Frank gently set the plane down, taxied to a short dock, and tied up next to a red and white Super Cub. The three passengers disembarked and followed a path that led from the dock to a well-maintained and somewhat luxurious log cabin. As they approached, a tired-looking man stuck his head out of the door and eyeballed his uninvited guests.

"Good morning. I assume you're Bryce Cameron," Bob said.

"That would be me. What's this about?"

"If you've got a few minutes we'd like to ask you some questions about your involvement with the Northwest Metals project."

"Oh, shit, what have they done now?"

"Can we come in for a minute?"

"OK. Please forgive the mess. I've been sick and cleanup hasn't been a high priority."

Bob introduced Charlie and JB and they all sat at a small dining room table overlooking the beautiful lake and mountains beyond. "So, what is your role on the project?" asked Bob.

"The way things have worked out, I haven't really had much of a role except for providing a whole shitload of money that I may never see again," replied Bryce.

"You don't sound happy. Can you explain how you got involved and why things aren't going well?" Charlie said.

"About a year ago a smooth-talking guy from Vancouver came to my office in Anchorage and asked if I would be interested in investing in a potentially very profitable gold mining venture south of here. He said that I could get triple my money back or more. He was very convincing and I stupidly agreed."

"Was his name Hank Gottfried by any chance?" asked JB.

"Yep, that's the guy. Anyway, they began setting up the exploration camp last fall and began core drilling this spring. Before they started, I sat in on an initial meeting with Gottfried and a mining engineer named Craig Johnson to discuss what was going to happen. I also gave them a large check at that time. Since then, in spite of my efforts, I have had almost no contact with them. I finally got through to Gottfried about a month ago and, though he admitted that initial exploration was not promising, he refused to give any indication where they were going to go from there. I've asked to visit the camp to see what my investment has bought, but they said that wasn't necessary. That's pretty much all I know. Personal problems have consumed my life in recent weeks, and I haven't had a chance to pursue things further. So, what's going on? It must be serious if you guys have come all the way out here."

"Is there anything about the operation that seems odd to you?" asked Bob.

"Well, yeah. They took my money and now they won't talk to me. That doesn't seem like a good sign. Plus, at the first meeting I went to, there was this creepy security guy named Max-something who was hovering around. He didn't say much, but he gave me an uneasy feeling. The worst of it is that my wife was pissed that I invested in such a risky venture, and now it seems that she was right."

Bob leaned closer to Bryce with a serious look. "One of the things that we are investigating is a trespass situation on the neighboring claim. It looks like Northwest Metals did some core drilling beyond the claim boundaries. Do you know anything about that?"

"No, but I guess I'm not too surprised. In my last discussion with Craig Johnson he implied that the exploration had been extended to the margins of the claim with less than stellar results."

"Unfortunately, the trespass is the least of it. Two geologists were murdered while working on their claim just to the east."

"Holy shit!" Bryce exclaimed with wide eyes. "I don't know anything about that. I'll admit to making some questionable business decisions, maybe even slightly shady, but violence is not part of who I am. I don't even like to kill fish. Do you guys think that the Northwest Metals people are involved in the murders?"

"Right now we're just gathering information," Bob answered. "We don't really know whether they're involved in the murders or not. Assuming that you are telling the truth, it might be best to keep quiet about our visit to protect your own safety."

"Wow. Things just keep going from bad to worse. I'm almost

bankrupt, my wife kicked me out, and now I may have accidentally become involved in some kind of criminal conspiracy. Do I need a lawyer?"

"You're not accused of anything, and there's no evidence of your involvement, so I wouldn't worry about a lawyer right now," Bob said.

"However," Charlie said slowly. "You may want to try to get your money back eventually, in which case a lawyer might be useful."

While Bob conducted the interview, Charlie and JB glanced around the cabin. Nothing outwardly suggested that Bryce was anything other than a depressed man trying to deal with life's unfortunate circumstances. However, throughout the interview Bryce had been fidgeting like a four-year-old who was too far from a bathroom. It was hard to tell whether his anxiety was due to guilt or his self-described personal crises.

As quickly as it had begun, their visit ended as they escorted themselves from Bryce's cabin and made their way back to the trooper-charted Beaver. As the plane took off from the calm lake, Charlie looked back and could see Bryce standing in the cabin doorway. Bryce's expression seemed worried and fearful rather than angry at the intrusion.

Chapter Twelve

Charlie and Kate were eating breakfast in the galley of the Shearwater when the call from Janine came in. "Some jerk broke into our office and trashed the place last night. What the hell is going on here? Why would anybody break into our office? What could we have that is so important to someone?" Janine explained that whoever broke in was obviously looking for something, but luckily she had put the files in the safe so nothing valuable had been taken. "Our office is a former jewelry store that happens to have a very secure safe built into the concrete floor."

"The intruder was probably expecting that the only security would be flimsy file cabinet locks, which are easy to break into. He must have been very annoyed when seeing the safe, especially one integrated into the floor. We need to take another careful look at the field notes. Obviously, somebody thinks there is something valuable there," Charlie said.

"The problem," suggested Kate, "is that none of us have enough knowledge of geology or mining engineering to determine what is important."

"Maybe JB knows someone who could help through his past association with a university," added Charlie after Janine had hung up.

"Did I hear my name mentioned?" said JB as he barged into the small galley and plopped down at the settee. JB's T-shirt du jour featured the Grateful Dead levitated above an outdoor concert stage along with the caption, *The dead can only improve.*

"Yeah. Do you know any geologists or mineral experts from your professorial days that we can consult?"

"Maybe. I have a former friend at USC who is normally pretty bored and would probably enjoy getting involved in an Alaskan adventure. I'll give him a call if I can find his number. I haven't talked to him in years."

Kate and Charlie informed JB about Janine's call and the break-in.

"Wow. The plot thickens. All this stuff screams of desperation or extreme greed on someone's part. I can't help but think that there must be something more to the story than competition between gold miners. There are gold prospects all over the state, but normally people don't go around killing each other," said JB.

"I don't suppose there are any video cameras that would shed light on the identity of the intruder," said Kate.

"I can ask the Super Trooper, but I doubt it," said Charlie. "Meanwhile, since I don't have anything going on this afternoon, I can take another look at the files. My Geology 101 background isn't going to get me very far, but maybe I can pick up on something that will give us a clue what the mystery man was after."

†

A couple hours later Charlie was sitting in the small conference room in the South Peninsula Gold office with a stack of field notebooks, maps, and aerial photos in front of him. He was starting to get some sense of Jeremy and Jason's approach to the surficial mineral exploration process. The geology of surface rock outcrops was combined with a look at the placer deposits in the small stream that flowed down the mountainside. Tests of stream deposits using gold pans had found some gold and platinum suggesting a mineral lode somewhere upstream, but the quantities were not exceptional. Rock samples from outcrops higher on the mountainside showed some quartz veins with associated microscopic gold flakes. However, Charlie knew that none of the findings were terribly unusual. During the gold rush period, almost every stream in the state had been sampled by prospectors, including the one at the SPG site, and traces of gold had been found in many of them. But in most cases the quantities were too small to make mining or panning worthwhile.

He was working on the fourth field book when he saw some notes on unusual alkaline rock formations with reference to one of the project maps where the location of the odd rock was noted. In the margin next to the field entry was scribbled the note: *"bring radiation meter on next trip."* When Janine came in to check on Charlie's progress, he asked her about the entry and whether Jeremy and Jason had taken a radiation detector with them on their fateful last trip.

"Yeah, they definitely had one since I rented it for them, and now I guess I'm going to have to replace it since you guys didn't find it in your cleanup of the campsite."

"Maybe your insurance will cover it. It's definitely interesting that we did not find the instrument when we searched the campsite. I can't imagine that we missed it. Did Jeremy say anything about why they needed the radiation detector?"

"No. But he seemed kind of excited by the whole thing."

"Do you mind if I copy some pages from the notebooks and let a geologist look at it?"

"No, go for it. But we probably should insist on confidentiality, especially if any of this stuff means the claim is actually worth something."

"I agree," Charlie said.

Charlie finished his review of the files, and he copied any

information that he thought might help provide some insight into the bizarre situation that had occurred at the claim. Returning to the harbor, he boarded the *Otterly Ridiculous* and woke JB from his habitual early afternoon siesta. JB scanned the copied files at his tiny desk in the bowels of the old boat and emailed them to Professor Ed Jackson in the geology department at USC. He then called the number at the college and was surprised when the phone was promptly answered by his friend.

"Johann, to what do I owe this unexpected call? I bet you want to pick my exceptional brain."

"Maybe I just wanted to talk to an old friend," replied JB. "But, as it turns out, I do need your expertise. I'm here with my friend, Charlie, and we have become embroiled in a situation where mineral value may be causing some people to behave very badly. I just emailed some notes from a geologist's field notebook, and I was wondering if you could take a quick look and give us an opinion on what the significance might be."

"OK. I'm opening the notes now. Is there some reason why you can't ask the author what it all means?"

"Yeah. He's dead."

"This is starting to get more interesting. From what I can see at a glance, it seems like the prospectors were most interested in gold and maybe other heavy metals, but some of the notations suggest that they may have stumbled on zones with potential for rare earth elements. The reference to alkaline rocks and other notes has nothing to do with gold, and the need for a radiation meter also hints at rare earth elements. Some of the elements, or the minerals with which they are associated, are radioactive, and the meter would be an obvious way of confirming their suspicions. If you have been following geopolitics in recent years, you know that rare earth elements have become vital components of many high-tech devices and new-generation batteries. China currently has a near monopoly on the most important of these elements."

"So, I assume that a significant find could be quite valuable," JB said.

"Yes, but there are some fourteen rare earth elements defined by their position in the periodic table. The chemistry, minerology, and refining are very complicated, and much more would need to be known before any prospect would be considered economically viable. If you want to know more about them, Wikipedia would be a good place to start, then maybe move on to a recent minerology textbook."

"Is the competition for these minerals intense enough that people would commit murder?" JB asked.

"Maybe. China is obviously vested in maintaining their stranglehold on the supply. Other countries including Canada and Greenland are trying to get in on the act. Future demand is almost certain to skyrocket."

JB described the events of the past days and Ed was amazed that such bizarre events would occur over competition for a mining claim. "Normally in a situation like that the two claim owners would simply combine forces and, if they got lucky, they would both become rich," replied Ed.

"What kind of information would be necessary to confirm the rare earth thing?" asked Charlie.

"You said that a core sample had surreptitiously been taken from the property. If you could get that sample and have it analyzed by a minerology lab, it could provide a better indication of the mineral potential. I might be willing to use our lab here to help out. It could become a student work project."

"If the level of desperation is as intense as it appears, it seems unlikely that Northwest Metals will hand over the samples. Or, if they do, they could substitute fake samples," JB said.

"Would it be possible to get information from drill cuttings brought up to the surface by the core drill?" asked Charlie.

"You could get some information – basic chemistry and radioactivity – but the vertical relationship between rock strata would be lost. Also there might be contamination with drill muds used to lubricate the drill bit. So, you would be looking at a soup of elements. Nevertheless, it might be worthwhile. If you could get me a cup of dirt from multiple samples around the bore hole, I could take a quick look at it. It would just take a few minutes to run the dirt through one of our atomic spectrum analyzers," replied Ed.

"That's an excellent idea. Plus, it would give us an excuse to go back over there," said JB with a devious smile.

†

Later that same day Lee Chen and Hank Gottfried sat in a separate back room of a restaurant in Vancouver's Chinatown. Few tourists patronized the inconspicuous establishment, but the restaurant was well known and very popular among Chinatown residents. Large platters of savory wok-fried meat and vegetable dishes were brought by an attractive young waitress along with a complementary pitcher of Tsingtao beer. Lee was a favored customer, and his known association with the Chinese underworld further guaranteed exceptional service and the prettiest waitresses.

"Last night Max Karelian broke into the South Peninsula Gold office in Homer looking for any information that would help us in our endeavors. Unfortunately, their files were apparently in a very secure safe that we were not expecting. He didn't find anything useful," said

Gottfried.

"That's unfortunate. I hope he did not leave any evidence," replied Lee.

"No, we should be in the clear, but the authorities will obviously suspect us. So, where should we go from here? Considering the amount of attention we're getting, maybe we should think about calling the whole project off."

"That is not an option," said Lee. "Preliminary results suggest that the underground resource is very valuable. My bosses would be most upset if the money they have spent so far was for nothing. I can't guarantee our safety if that should happen."

"Well, that's just great," replied Gottfried with a panicked look on his face. "It would have helped if I had known the stakes when I first took this job."

"Stop whining, Mr. Gottfried. I'm afraid you will have to deal with it."

"Yeah, yeah. By the way, did you order Karelian to kill the guys on the claim next door?"

"I asked him to apply some pressure to help convince them to sell, but somehow things got out of hand. Maybe the two men fought back or insulted Karelian. But we can't change things now. We made a mistake hiring such a volatile individual. But there is no direct evidence connecting us to the murders, so we have only broken the trespass laws. We need to keep going with this summer's exploration."

As Hank Gottfried tried to choke down his cashew chicken given the unsettling nature of the conversation, he began to wonder whether Lee Chen was completely anchored to reality. Intimidation may be an effective strategy within the Chinese autocracy but might not work very well in the U.S. He did not think that the Alaskan authorities would simply forget about the murders. Hank was beginning to understand that he was completely screwed. It would be dangerous to continue with the NBM consortium, and it would be dangerous to attempt to leave the project.

His career had started out well with his special expertise managing projects for far eastern clients, but it had taken a very unfortunate turn. He had gone from successful businessman to potential fugitive in the blink of an eye. He started to think about possible escape plans, maybe obtaining new identities for himself and his family. Warm climates were starting to sound very appealing.

Chapter Thirteen

White, frothy water cascaded down the mountainside, coating the stream-side vegetation with a fine mist. The morning sun was beginning to shine over the top of a ridge, creating bright sun spots between the scraggly spruce trees. A pair of pikas whistled warning notes from the talus slope above. Once again Charlie and JB hiked up toward the illegal core drill site. They could hear helicopter activity from the Northwest Metals claim area, but the topography prevented them from seeing the choppers. As they climbed the final plateau near the site, the view to the east opened up, presenting a panoramic view of Cook Inlet, its waters shimmering in the morning light. A large container ship cruised up the middle of the estuary on its way to the Anchorage port with supplies for the entire state. Beyond the ship, the west shore of the Kenai Peninsula was visible in the distance.

At the drill site they scooped up dirt from around the bore hole and put it into two clean sample bottles. "Since we're already through with our primary task, I suggest we conduct a little stealth surveillance on our neighbors," JB said.

"I completely agree. Lead the way."

JB headed west and down into the trees, his gangly frame seeming to glide across the rugged terrain. As Charlie followed, he wondered, not for the first time, how JB's athleticism squared with his awkward appearance and reportedly nerdy background. After an hour of difficult walking, they broke over the top of a minor ridge that provided an expansive view of the Northwest Metals camp and surrounding valley. A helicopter was in the process of lifting a sling load of timbers from the camp staging area before it flew off to the south and dropped its load at a presumed drill site on a slope at the edge of the valley. The chopper then returned to the camp, landed, and shut off its engine. The pilot entered the command tent. All was quiet for about twenty minutes.

"Well, this is pretty boring. Everybody must be eating lunch," JB said.

"Yeah. They seem to be doing what they are supposed to be doing. Wait a second. I hear an incoming chopper," replied Charlie as they both dove under the bushes. Suddenly, a loud black helicopter with white swooshy stripes thundered over the ridge and right over their heads.

"Crap," Charlie exclaimed with his face in a blueberry bush. "I hope they didn't see us."

But the machine continued on and set down on the camp helicopter pad. Charlie and JB retrieved binoculars from their packs and focused on the parked machine. Three people disembarked and walked toward the command tent. At the same time, Craig Johnson and Max Karelian came out to meet them. The pilot remained in his seat.

"Wow. One of those guys is Asian, probably Chinese," JB said. "From the appearance of the other two men, it looks like one may be a Caucasian business type, and the other has the mannerisms of a body guard."

The "body guard" and Max Karelian greeted each other, shook hands, and walked off to the side. Their behavior suggested that they knew each other. The others entered the command tent. The pilot exited the helicopter and went behind a bush to relieve himself. As he returned back to the chopper, Charlie was able to get a good look at his face.

"The pilot also looks Asian. Since the helicopter is a very expensive model with a custom paint job, it might be a reasonable guess that the machine is corporate-owned, rather than a charter."

JB was watching the two apparent security men. The man from the chopper pointed up to where Charlie and JB were watching. "Oh, oh," JB said. "I think they may know we're here. I vote for moving farther back into the trees."

As they retreated, they heard four gunshots and simultaneous sound of bullets ripping through the foliage above their heads. Diving for cover JB said, "They know they can't hit us with pistols at this range, and they don't know exactly where we are, so the shots were just intended to scare us. I'd like to see the look on the other guys' faces when they find out their security thugs are shooting at a hillside. Let's sneak back out to where we can see what's going on."

Charlie and JB circled around to a different viewing location being careful to stay hidden. They were in time to see Craig Johnson wildly gesticulating to Max Karelian. Although they could not hear what was being said, it was obvious that an argument was in progress. The Asian man stood to the side and did not participate. After talking for a few minutes, all the men re-entered the camp headquarters.

"Looks like all is not peaceful in gold mining world," JB said.

"Yeah. I'm starting to wonder whether there may be competing agendas. Let's call it a day," Charlie said.

Charlie and JB retraced their path through the mining claims, stopping periodically to listen for pursuing helicopters. Fortunately, no pursuit was forthcoming. They reached the South Peninsula Gold property without incident, descended to the shoreline, boarded their borrowed speedboat, and returned to Homer. They reached town in time to drop off the soil samples at the FedEx office for next-day delivery to southern California.

Chapter Fourteen

The next morning dawned cold and rainy. The drumbeat of large drops on the pilothouse roof and rhythmic dripping from the rigging created an annoying amount of noise. The world outside the pilothouse windows consisted of shades of gray – gray ocean, gray mountains, and gray clouds. But inside the boat it was warm and cozy. Buster the cat was draped fluidly on the counter next to the stove. Kate and Charlie were eating breakfast before Kate had to head to work.

"So, you said that the helicopter at the camp yesterday had distinctive markings. Maybe Mike at Kachemak Choppers has seen the bird around someplace," suggested Kate. "There is a fair chance that the machine is based in Alaska, since it is expensive and logistically complicated to arrange fuel stops for a trip from the lower forty-eight."

After Kate left for work, Charlie called Mike and asked about the mysterious black helicopter with white markings that looked like the logo from an athletic shoe company. Mike said that he had seen a machine matching that description once at a mine site in the Alaskan interior. He thought it was owned by a small company called Mercury Transport based in Wasilla, north of Anchorage.

"Did you meet any of the pilots?" asked Charlie.

"Not really. I sat near one of the guys at the camp mess hall, but he was apparently not interested in conversation."

"What was his nationality?"

"He looked Asian, maybe Chinese."

"Do you have any idea what role Mercury Transport played in the mine operation?'"

"Well, they definitely weren't the primary helicopter contractor. Another company was involved with the day-to-day chopper needs. They may have been delivering supplies or special machine parts, like I was. Expediting delivery of critical machine parts is a major headache for remote Alaska mines and provides a lot of business for helicopter companies. Often mine-company expediters simply choose the most convenient and available transport. Even though helicopters are expensive, a work stoppage may be more expensive, given the high wages paid to the workers."

Charlie Googled Mercury Transport and found a bare-bones web site that described the company as providing support for the mining industry. Their home office was apparently in Australia, with branch offices in several mine-intensive areas including northern Canada, New Mexico, Alaska, and Indonesia. No information was available regarding ownership or the names of personnel. The mention of several projects in Southeast Asia and the South China Sea suggested a possible Asian origin.

As Charlie was wrapping up his internet search, he saw JB emerge from the cave that was the below-deck cabin of the *Otterly Ridiculous*. Seconds later he vaulted onto the deck of the Shearwater and joined Charlie at the little dinette in the pilothouse.

"So, JB. What do you think we should do about being shot at yesterday?"

"I don't know. Were we technically trespassing?"

"My understanding of mining law is that patented mining claims are considered private property, and, therefore, we were technically trespassing. Mining claim laws were established in the 1870s, and many consider the laws obsolete. I'm not sure what the law would say about those guys shooting at us. It certainly wasn't very neighborly.

Maybe we should avoid mentioning the episode to Bob. He might not approve of our clumsy methods," replied Charlie.

"On the other hand, maybe Bob could use their over-the-top aggressiveness as a lever to get cooperation from Northwest Metals."

"Yeah. Let's see how things play out in the next few days."

†

Later that afternoon JB was working at his tiny desk and his phone rang. "Professor Jackson, I wasn't expecting to hear from you so soon. What's going on?"

"I got your soil samples this morning, and my students ran them through the analyzer right away. I'll email a full report tomorrow with technical details. The results were pretty interesting. As expected, the drill cuttings were a mix of rock types from different vertical strata, but there were definitely some indications of rare-earth minerology plus some low-level radioactivity, so our initial suspicions were probably correct. It's not possible to speculate about the economic value without knowing more about the composition and distribution of the rare-earth ore. My guess is that there is some gold-bearing rock in the strata above the potential rare-earth strata. We really need to get our hands on some of the core samples."

"Wow, Ed. Thanks for the quick turnaround. I'm not sure where we go from here. I don't see any way to get the core samples without breaking and entering, and, even then, the samples are so heavy and bulky that we would need a helicopter to get them out."

"Since the samples were obtained illegally to begin with, would it be possible to force Northwest Base Metals to get them out for you?" asked Ed.

"Maybe. But we would have no way of determining whether they were the right samples. Unfortunately, I don't think South Peninsula Gold has the will or the resources right now to do any of their own core drilling," replied JB.

"Anyway, if you are able to get more information and more samples, my students and I would be happy to help out. This is a pretty interesting situation. Keep me posted."

"Thanks a lot for your help. I'll report back if we ever figure any of this out."

Chapter Fifteen

Late the following afternoon the three mooseketeers were back in the galley of the Shearwater, trying to make sense of everything that had happened. The weather had turned unpleasant, with a cold rain noisily beating an irregular rhythm on the deck and gusty winds pushing the boat back and forth against its mooring lines. Outside the harbor, the bay was whipped up into frothy whitecaps. The galley seemed especially cozy in contrast to the outside conditions. Beer and chips served to lubricate the conversation.

"So," Kate said slowly, her face tense with concentration, "it looks like there are some dangerous and desperate people out there who may, or may not, be associated with the adjoining mining claim, and may, or may not, be somehow associated with Chinese mining interests. But murdering two people and breaking and entering at South Peninsula Gold seem like unnecessarily desperate measures. Even if there is intense interest in the potential for rare earth commodities, there have got to be better ways to achieve their goals."

"I agree. There's got to be another angle to this," replied Charlie.

"Maybe it revolves around personal ambition rather than corporate competition. It's easier to imagine an individual reaching such an extreme point of desperation than an entire corporation. Maybe a frustrated upper-level employee feels pressure to succeed and will do anything to get there," Kate said.

"Or maybe the Chinese government is desperate to maintain its competitive edge in the world markets. Their history of industrial espionage indicates that they are willing to do illegal stuff, especially if it means embarrassing the United States. Presumably, the troopers are looking into the corporation so maybe Bob can give us some more information," Charlie said. "In the meantime, what do we do?"

"One thing I would like to do is get a look inside that little metal building at the mine camp," said JB.

"How do you propose to do that? Setting aside the fact that the place is hard to get to, looking inside that building would involve trespassing and breaking and entering," replied Kate.

"I was thinking I could hike to the NBM camp and do an after-dark reconnaissance. I'm a pretty sneaky guy. In a past life I was trained to do exactly that kind of thing," said JB.

"Oh, great. What if you get caught, and what do you expect to find?" added Kate.

"Come on, I won't get caught," replied JB. "I don't know what's in the building, but it seemed odd to me that there would be a separate locked, hard-sided building at a remote camp where all the other structures are basically fancy tents. As far as I could tell, the core samples were stored in the main office tent along with documents and computers. So, what do they need to hide?"

"I sort of agree with JB," Charlie chimed in. "But it may not be worth the risk. We should probably get an update from the Super Trooper before we do anything. Let's meet with Bob tomorrow morning,"

"OK. But for now, I'm really hungry. Let's get something to eat." said Kate.

"You're always hungry," teased JB.

†

After finishing his twelve-hour shift on the drilling crew, Travis crossed the yard and entered the Quonset hut that he shared with three other drillers. As usual the hut was filled with cigarette smoke, one of the worst aspects of his job at the NBM exploration site. His fellow workers left much to be desired. They were all scruffy and heavily bearded, as was Travis. He had avoided haircuts, grown a full beard, and collected used work clothes prior to starting the job – all attempts to fit in with the culture of remote-camp construction workers. His training as a foreman of the core drilling crew and falsified résumé had been courtesy of his uncle, Lee Chen. Although Lee was his uncle, Travis was only one quarter Chinese and his overall appearance was mostly Caucasian.

Travis reclined on his bunk and waited for the other members of the crew to leave for the mess hall and a well-deserved dinner. When the coast was clear, he quietly exited the hut and headed on a back trail through the trees to the mysterious little building at the edge of the compound. He knew that the professional staff were out observing a new drill site, the cook was busy with dinner, and the clerical assistant was busy typing notes.

The specially equipped metal building was about eight feet square with eight foot ceilings. It had been prefabricated offsite and airlifted into the camp months earlier by a large helicopter. Travis unlocked the door, entered the building, and turned on battery-powered lights. He sat at a small bench on the right side, and powered up a computer. On the bench next to him were a satellite phone and expensive radio equipment. The inside of the building was isolated from radio or satellite signals, but the equipment inside was connected to special antennas built into the roof. On the left side was another bench with various metallurgical instruments, as well as an apparatus reminiscent of high school chemistry class.

After the computer booted up, Travis opened an encrypted message site and saw that he had a note from his uncle asking him to call as soon as possible. Using the encrypted satphone, Travis dialed.

"What's going on uncle?" said Travis when the call went through.

"It seems like things have been exciting up there. What is the status of the police investigation?"

"The cops haven't visited the camp again, but the other day a couple of guys were seen snooping on the ridge above camp. The out-of-control mercenaries that you hired fired a couple of pistol shots at them. I'm afraid that will only draw more attention to the operation."

"I agree that was very foolish. But don't worry about the murders. You won't be implicated. There's no evidence connecting you or anyone else to them. Please try to relax. What's happening with the exploration?"

"We started drilling at a new site today. Craig thinks it may have some potential for gold, but I think he is starting to understand that there may be other minerals here. Anyway, I'll get some pieces from the new cores and run them through the analyzers."

Belying his appearance as a scruffy drill operator, Travis had a master's degree in minerology from Stanford. He was well aware of the geopolitical aspects of mineral development and international competition for the most valuable minerals.

†

On the following day, an early morning meeting of sorts was taking place at a bakery/café on the outskirts of Homer. Kate, Charlie, JB, and Bob Stillwater were sitting at a table at the back of the establishment. Bob's prodigious bulk was occupying one whole side of the table. A large carafe of coffee and a plate of mixed pastries were strategically placed in front of Kate and JB.

"I assume you guys are going to interfere with my investigation once again," groaned Bob.

"I prefer to think of it as assisting our dedicated and overworked law enforcement officers," said JB as he reached for a pastry.

"OK. So, what ideas do you geniuses have?"

Charlie filled Bob in on the trip that he and JB had made to the SPG claim, the collection of samples from the drill cuttings, and the possible value of rare earth elements. They omitted being shot at by NBM guys.

"Do you have any new information since we last talked?" asked Charlie.

"A little. We've been trying to get a better idea of the ownership of Northwest Base Metals, but the corporate structure is layered with secrecy. One of our financial crimes guys is working to penetrate the veil. The ME did manage to find a 9 mm bullet lodged against Jason Biele's spine, but there were no matches with existing ballistics databases," replied Bob.

"I hesitate to mention this with a law enforcement person in the room, but I was considering making a surreptitious reconnaissance of the NBM camp with emphasis on determining the purpose of the small metal building," added JB.

"I didn't hear that," said Bob.

"Me either," said Kate. "Especially since it sounds really dangerous and stupid, not to mention illegal."

"It sounds like fun to me," chuckled JB before sinking his teeth into his pastry.

Chapter Sixteen

Once again JB found himself hiking through the spruce forest on the west side of Cook Inlet. Arriving at the South Peninsula Gold claim area at mid-morning after crossing the inlet in a borrowed boat, his plan was to make his way to the NBM claim area by evening, observe and wait until about midnight, then surreptitiously investigate anything needing investigating. He carried a light backpack containing food, water, assorted spy stuff, and other gear that would allow him to stay comfortable during his long wait. In his jacket pocket he carried his favorite weapon – a small, chrome-plated Beretta pistol in .32 caliber. The little gun was not as accurate or as powerful as contemporary law enforcement weapons, but JB still liked it. The gun had sentimental value since it had saved his butt on several occasions in the distant past. He had no intention of actually using the gun unless he was in a clear self-defense situation. Gunfire would obviously defeat his whole purpose for being there.

It was a beautiful day and the forest was alive with life. Red squirrels raced around like adolescents with ADHD, gathering spruce cones and stashing them for later use. JB wondered how they remembered the locations of their many hidey holes. Most of the early summer bird song had ended, but thrushes and some warblers continued to sing. Hordes of mosquitos and black flies tended to offset the pleasant bird song.

Using the navigation functions on his phone, JB set a course directly from the beach to the NBM campsite, a distance of about seven miles through forest and over several ridges. In most places the forest canopy was dense resulting in total shade, but in other areas dappled sun light pierced the canopy, creating varying and contrasting shades of green from moss and leaves, as well as gray and white from the bark of spruce and birch. Dust motes danced in the rays of light. Some of the old gnarled birch trees looked almost like trolls in an enchanted German forest.

Unfortunately, the hiking was very difficult. Dead spruce windfall caused by a bark beetle infestation fifteen years earlier made it impossible to go in a straight line. Impenetrable thickets of random branches and horizontal tree trunks made wide detours mandatory. He remembered training years earlier in the swamps of Georgia where he was tasked to go from point A to point B regardless of what might be in the way. While the Alaskan forest was ecologically much different, the mental strain was similar. JB tried to assume a familiar Zen-like resolve allowing him to continually push forward without dwelling on how miserable he was. He finally arrived within sight of the camp at about seven o'clock. He found a comfortable, but hidden, observation post, and settled in for a long wait.

The twelve-hour shift was just ending and workers were being shuttled by helicopter back into camp for the night. JB tried to gather as much information as possible about the number, function, and ethnicity of the workers. It looked like there were about a dozen drillers, a couple of camp housekeeping staff, along with the professional staff that JB had met earlier. There was nothing obviously remarkable about the drillers. They were scruffy, dirty, and tired, as would be expected at the end of a long shift wrangling a mud-slinging diamond drill. As far as JB could tell, the non-professional workers were housed in three of the Quonset structures, each of which accommodated four or five people. Most of the workers took a few minutes to clean up and then went directly to dinner at the common mess hall. Dinner is the highlight of the day for workers at remote camps, and eating is taken seriously. The food is expected to be good, and the competition for skilled camp cooks is fierce. Worker mutiny has been known to cause poor cooks to be forcibly run out of remote camps.

JB reclined in his nest with binoculars trained on the action. He munched on jerky and granola bars while maintaining his watch. About ten minutes after most of the workers had gone to dinner, he noticed a lone individual leave one of the driller tents and work his way around the back of the camp clearing. He watched the man approach and enter the mysterious little metal building and close the door. The man had no real distinctive features; he was white, average height, and had a full dark beard. Because of the beard and a baseball cap it was hard to get a good look at his face. JB was somewhat surprised since he had been expecting the unfriendly security guy, Max Karelian, to be the wild card at the camp. But it was looking like this other guy was also playing a role. At a minimum he was more than just a driller. The mystery man remained in the little building for about twenty minutes before quickly and quietly leaving and heading towards the mess hall.

A short time later most of the workers finished dinner and gradually made their way back to their sleeping quarters. A few men hung around outside, smoking cigarettes and socializing. All normal stuff. After nine o'clock everything was quiet, and camp was mostly deserted except for the helicopter mechanic doing his nightly maintenance. Unfortunately, JB still had to wait a couple of hours for it to get dark because of the long summer light period.

JB had dozed off but woke with a start at about eleven when he heard voices. In the dimming light he was able to see two men about a hundred feet from his location. They were standing still and talking in hushed tones. JB was certain that one of the men was Max Karelian because of the stocky build and dark clothing. The other man might have been the same guy that he had seen earlier go into the mystery building, but he could not be sure. The items in JB's backpack included a directional microphone and recording device capable of picking up conversations from several hundred feet away. He fumbled to get it out and functioning. Through headphones he was able to make out some of the conversation, which seemed to be picking up in volume and emotion.

"Mr. Chen is not happy with the fact that you guys shot at visitors. We don't need any more attention than we've already got. I'm not sure if shooting at claim intruders is strictly legal, but it probably doesn't matter. The incident gives law enforcement an excuse to investigate further."

"I don't give a shit what you and Mr. Chen think. I don't answer to you."

"Maybe you don't answer to me, but you do answer to the people paying for all this, and Lee Chen is currently their representative. Things are going to be very sensitive for a while because of the murders, so we need to be careful and keep a low profile. Meanwhile, tell me about the break-in at South Peninsula gold."

"There's not much to tell. It was a complete bust. Nobody told me that there was a heavy-duty safe built into the floor."

"That was bad luck. Is there any chance it could get tied to you?"

"I don't think so. There were no cameras, no witnesses, and I didn't leave any evidence."

The two men walked back to their quarters. JB settled back into his hiding place to wait until total darkness. Clouds had moved in, which promised a dark night.

Two hours later, JB's phone alarm vibrated and he awoke again. Donning night-vision goggles, he stood up, looked around, and, seeing no one, started his sneaky reconnaissance. On a whim several weeks earlier, he had purchased various items from an online spy store, mostly because he thought they were cool. It was coincidental that the items were being put to use so quickly. During a former life he had used older-generation night-vision equipment, and he was very impressed by how much they had improved in the intervening years. The camp and surrounding forest appeared as varying shades of green. Resolution was amazingly good. He could see no living beings.

JB moved slowly and quietly around the edge of the cleared area, eventually coming to the mysterious metal building. A small amount of light leaking under the bottom of the door almost blinded him because of the sensitivity of the light amplification device. Pushing the goggles up on his forehead, he realized the strong possibility that someone was in the structure. Maybe this was a lucky break, but only if he could get an idea what the person was doing. He could hear no sound but suspected that the building was well insulated. JB moved silently to a back corner near the trees out of sight of the front door and put his ear against the wall. He thought he could hear some clinking noises, sort of like glass striking a hard surface. The sound amplifier that he used with the directional microphone also had a feature allowing direct contact with a hard surface. Placing the amplifier against the wall and putting on headphones, he was able to hear the sounds more clearly from inside the structure. He heard the shuffling feet of someone moving around, more clinking, paper crumpling, liquid dripping, and some metallic sounds. JB searched his sound memory banks but could not put the sounds together into a coherent activity. He really wanted to get into the building.

Obviously, he would have to wait until the occupant left the premises. JB moved a few feet back into the woods behind a shrub to wait once again. Fifteen minutes later, the door opened accompanied by a burst of light. The light clicked off, the door was shut and locked, and the mystery man walked away. JB quickly pulled his goggles back over his eyes and tried to get a look at the dark figure. The profile suggested the same guy as before, but he could not be sure.

After a few minutes, JB scanned the area to make sure all was clear and moved to the doorway. The lock was commercial quality, but JB thought he could probably open it. Reaching into his bag of tricks, he pulled out a lock-picking kit and went to work. It was challenging, but he finally managed to open the door. He went in, closed and locked the door, placed his extra jacket along the bottom of the door to block any escaping light, and flipped the light switch. He saw that the small room contained instruments and labware on one side and communications equipment on the other. JB photographed everything including labels on reagent bottles, book titles, and model numbers for radio and phone gear. A dish of sandy dirt was sitting on the lab counter. JB poured a small sample of the dirt into a clean vial and put it into his pocket. It suddenly clicked that the activity he heard through the wall was probably the mystery man conducting some kind of lab test.

Directing his attention to the bench on the right, he lifted the lid on the laptop computer, which immediately booted up. A password was required and he did not have time to mess with it, so he closed it back up. Also on the bench was a smartphone that was beefed up to also have satellite capability and an input for an external antenna. JB pushed the power button on the phone and was surprised to see that it was not password protected. Scrolling through various menu options allowed JB to view contacts, recent calls, email, and anything else on the phone. He photographed every screen that he thought would be useful including several pages of emails.

So far, his reconnaissance had been far more productive than he could have hoped. But he thought it would be really good if he could record phone conversations within the building. He was sure that the metal building was designed as a Faraday cage, blocking radio transmissions from within and without. Wires ran from each of the communication devices to the ceiling where, he assumed, they were connected to external antennas. His bag of tricks included a voice-activated recording device that was capable of transmitting audio recordings via satellite phone, but he could not figure out how to get the signal outside the cage.

JB was starting to get nervous about the amount of time he was spending in the enemy lair and was about to leave when he glanced at the ceiling and noticed a panel in the corner where antenna wires were routed. Hoping that everyone in camp was sleeping, given that they had to work twelve-hour shifts the next day, he decided to spend a few minutes to see if installing the recorder was a viable idea. Using a multi-tool, he loosened four screws from the panel corners and removed the panel. Inside was plenty of space to hide the recorder, but it still needed to be connected to the outside. One of the cables was coaxial, and so tapping in would be difficult and would likely affect its normal use. But another of the wires was a standard copper conductor and might serve the purpose. JB scraped insulation off a small segment of the wire and tightly wrapped the tiny wire from the recorder around it. JB powered up the recorder and replaced the panel having no idea whether it would actually work. He quickly packed his stuff, turned off the light, pulled his goggles over his eyes, and opened the door slowly. No one was in sight. Fortunately, the door had a lock button on the inside, so he just closed it behind him.

Retracing his steps around the perimeter of the camp, he almost ran into the helicopter mechanic who was apparently walking back to his tent after finishing his nightly maintenance. Fortunately, he saw the mechanic in time to duck behind a tree, and the clueless mechanic continued on his way. Reaching the east end of the camp clearing, JB re-entered the forest and began the long trek back to the boat. By the time he was a mile or so beyond the camp, light began to filter through the trees from the impending sunrise, accompanied by bird song and the stirrings of small forest creatures. It was a beautiful morning. The journey back was leisurely and much more pleasant than his initial hike into the camp. He even stopped to watch a beaver engaged in dam-repair work. The animal was carrying sticks to the breach and cementing them with mud scooped up with its tail. The pudgy animal had to battle constantly to maintain the water level in his pond, thus ensuring that the entrance to his house of sticks be far enough under water to prevent access by predators.

JB managed to reach the boat by midday and was back in Homer in time for a much-needed nap.

Chapter Seventeen

At four o'clock the next afternoon JB had not emerged from his bunk. Charlie was going nuts wanting to know what JB had found. JB had texted that he was back in Homer with exciting news, but he required a nap before a debriefing. A short time later Charlie noticed the mast of the *Otterly Ridiculous* jiggling and JB emerging from the companionway. He was even more disheveled than usual. His T-shirt of the day had an image of the Grateful Dead in which Jerry Garcia was surrounded by a purple aura.

"James Bond returns," remarked Charlie as JB came aboard and helped himself to a beer from Charlie's little refrigerator. "What did you learn?"

"I learned a lot. The problem is we're in the same situation as our last adventure. We have incriminating information, but most of it was illegally obtained and inadmissible in court. So somehow we need to feed stuff to the Super Trooper without acknowledging how we got it."

"Yeah, we'll have to think about that. Kate should be here any minute and you can fill us in. Meanwhile, I assume you survived. How was your hike through the untrammeled forest?"

"It was sort of exhausting, not to mention spending most of the night lying on the ground. I'm getting too old for this shit."

"It was your idea," Charlie added.

The boat rocked as Kate came on board after yet another exciting day of administrative paperwork at FlashFrozen. "I was worried about you," said Kate as she hugged JB and grabbed potato chips and a beer. "So what's the scoop?"

JB related his adventure and inferences regarding the rogue mining operation. He showed them the vial of sandy stuff that he purloined from the mini lab in the mystery building. "So, the bottom line is there is definitely something strange going on. It seems like the man I saw going into the mystery building is more than a driller. I'm betting that this vial contains ground-up rock from one of their better drill holes. I can send it to my geologist friend for analysis. I can also send him the photos of the lab equipment to see if they give him any insight into the kinds of analyses going on. I have no idea whether the audio recorder that I planted is going to work, but I can call it from my satphone late tonight and see if it connects. Probably best to call when no one is likely to be there since I don't know whether it will make any noise during the process. Obviously, it wouldn't be good if they found it. But the phone numbers found on the satphone may be the most valuable information we have."

"Wow," Charlie said with a look of surprise. "That was amazingly successful. I admit that I was skeptical when you first suggested it. I guess we should process the stuff we've got and then decide where to go from there."

"This may be a good time for me to try out my new hacking skills," Kate said. "I can check out the phone numbers as well as any names that we've uncovered. Maybe look into the corporate structure some more."

"I'll run the dirt sample in to FedEx before they close," said JB.

"By the way, JB, when is Beverly arriving?" asked Kate.

"Tomorrow morning at ten sharp."

"Awesome. The whole team will be back together just in time to help solve another murder."

"I'm really not sure that's what she has in mind," replied JB with a lecherous wink.

†

The Twin Otter commuter plane from Anchorage landed smoothly and taxied to the terminal at the small Homer International Airport. JB stood just inside the door to the baggage claim area and watched through the windows as Beverly disembarked. He was uncharacteristically excited, partly from pure lust since it had been a long winter, but mostly from anticipation of the fact that his life might be entering a new phase – one that included a real relationship with a member of the opposite sex. JB had had many short-term girlfriends, all of which ended up on very friendly terms. It was a mystery to Charlie how this could be the case since his own love affairs always ended badly. Apparently it had become a rite of passage for various female members of the Homer counterculture to spend quality time with JB, who was viewed as some sort of love guru.

As Beverly approached, JB admired her compact physique and fine facial features. She could best be described as cute. While not beautiful in the conventional sense, Beverly had a very expressive face, freckles, sparkling blue eyes, and short disheveled blonde hair. In short, she looked nothing like the stereotype of a stern female narcotics agent, except for her very fit body and tight butt, which JB found himself ogling in spite of himself. JB knew from their past adventures that her pleasant and friendly exterior concealed a bulldog mentality and a serious toughness. It probably would not be good to get on Beverly's bad side.

Beverly had started out as a fairly normal California girl. She studied accounting in college and worked in an accounting firm for several years before discovering that it was about as boring as watching grass grow. Needing a total change, she applied to the Drug Enforcement Agency, survived their academy, and went to work with the DEA in Los Angeles. Ironically, her experience as an accountant proved valuable in tracking money laundering related to drug trafficking and terrorism.

Beverly ran to JB and jumped into his arms in spite of their location in the crowded airport lobby. After collecting luggage, they walked hand in hand to JB's car. "OK, JB. What is this rumor I heard about you guys finding more dead bodies? Can't we just have a normal vacation together without worrying about solving crimes?"

"Well, probably not," replied JB. "Charlie and Kate are waiting for us on the boat, and we were hoping that you could help us with the situation."

"Of course you were," said Beverly.

JB described the events of the past few days as they drove to the harbor. Beverly groaned internally. The dangerous events of the previous year had been stressful. But she had to admit that she enjoyed working with Charlie, JB, and Kate, and the whole experience had been stimulating and ultimately rewarding – most of the bad guys had ended up in jail or otherwise out of commission. And it was a lot less boring than sitting in her LA office looking at bank accounts.

After hugs all around, it was as if Beverly had never left. She assumed her position next to JB on the settee surrounding the small galley table across from Kate and Charlie.

"So, Beverly, are you here for good?" asked Kate.

"Yeah, I've sort of already left the DEA. Technically, I'm still an employed law enforcement officer because I'm using banked vacation time, but I've given notice and won't be going back there. Basically,

I've formally resigned from the Drug Enforcement Agency, and I guess I'm joining JB in Homer for better or worse," replied Beverly.

"Let's hope it's not for worse," quipped Charlie.

"Speaking of worse," said Beverly. "Let me get this straight. You guys found two murder victims who may, or may not, be connected to a rogue mining enterprise based in Vancouver which may, or may not, be part of a criminal conspiracy involving Chinese mining interests? Plus, you've enlisted my boyfriend's special skills to investigate things in a wholly illegal manner?"

"That's about right, except your boyfriend enlisted himself in spite of our objections. Maybe we should talk about what this treasure trove of new information from JB's excursion across the inlet may tell us?" said Charlie as he spread maps and aerial photos on the table. Kate pulled up Google Earth on her laptop so Beverly could understand the geography of the situation.

"Kate, what did you find out about the phone numbers on the satphone recent calls list?"

"I took a quick look without employing the full range of my awesome new hacking skills. The number called the most often is an unlisted landline in Vancouver, BC."

"OK, here we go," said Beverly. "You guys are going to ask me to risk my job to trace a phone number."

"You've already given notice," remarked JB. "What have you got to lose?"

"Before Beverly risks pissing off her boss, let me see what I can find out," said Kate. "I need to get some practice in the world of cyber snooping."

"Wow, you guys are employing the full suite of illegal investigation activities," remarked Beverly. "How did I manage to get involved with a group of scofflaws?"

"Getting back to the original question," interjected Kate, "the only other number in the list was to a Molly Chen, also in Vancouver. A Google search of Molly suggests that she is a high school teacher, and images from Facebook suggested she is Caucasian, so she may be married to an Asian man. Nothing the least bit suspicious about Miss Chen except that there are no photos of her partner, assuming that there is one."

"OK, that's interesting," Charlie said. "What do you know, JB?"

"I called the voice recorder in the mystery building last night at about three a.m. It sounded like it connected but there was nothing recorded. Or, alternatively, it may not be working at all. On a more interesting note, I got an email from Professor Jackson. He said that the dirt we sent him was pretty hot stuff with definite potential for a commercial find. The apparatus and chemicals in the building could have been used for some very basic testing for rare earth minerals, but the *pièce de résistance* was a radiation meter with a label tape that said *Denali Geotechnical Supplies* on it. I bet it came from the ill-fated South Peninsula Gold campsite. If so, it would be pretty incriminating."

"Wow. I'll check with Janine to see if that's where she rented the meter," said Charlie. "Meanwhile, what the heck do we do with all this stuff? How can we convert this to enough legitimate evidence so that Bob can justify a surprise search warrant?"

"My personal opinion," Beverly added, "is that it is going to be difficult to get law enforcement involved, excluding me of course, with what we know so far. During our last adventure Charlie fed information to the troopers using the Crime Stoppers hot line. But this is a different situation. Bob probably won't be able to get a warrant based only on anonymous hearsay that there is incriminating stuff in a building at a mine site. Bob could use the information to continue his investigation, which he will probably do anyway, but if he continues to push, the radiation meter and anything else will disappear. The remote location of the claim further complicates things. Plus, any audio recording that JB might get would be illegally obtained. In fact, the device itself is illegal. Where did you get it, anyway?"

"I'm not telling," said JB. "Boy, you sure know how to put a damper on a perfectly good illegal investigation."

"I guess right now we've got other stuff to think about. Why don't we all ponder this stuff and get together tomorrow morning?" said Charlie.

"Excellent idea. Come on, JB. We've got other things to do," added Beverly.

JB's eyes lit up.

Chapter Eighteen

Kate decided to take matters into her own hands. She was sick of being left out of the most interesting stuff because she had to work while the rest of the mooseketeers goofed off. Plus, she wanted to see what she could do with her newly acquired hacking skills. She took a well-deserved personal day from FlashFrozen, settled into a comfortable spot at the galley table, told Charlie to leave her alone, and fired up her laptop. Her brother, James, had suggested various approaches to digging up information using both the regular search engines as well as the dark web and other overlay networks that are not easily accessible to the average user. James had warned her about the dark web and provided software to protect her identity. He had provided hints for breaking into supposedly secure systems. Additionally, he had given Kate bootlegged access information and credentials to one of the subscription-only commercial databases used by lawyers, law enforcement, and private detectives. In short, Kate had all the ammunition she needed to ferret out information. She just needed to be pointed in the right direction.

She started with what she thought might be the easiest inquiry – the unlisted landline phone number that JB had obtained from the satphone in the mystery building. She emailed her brother asking for advice on the best way to unmask the unlisted landline number in Vancouver. He responded quickly with suggestions on the best way to approach the problem. A half hour later Kate had managed to hack into the Vancouver phone utility system and discover that the number was registered to a Lee Chen with an office in Vancouver's Chinatown. Lee Chen and Molly Chen were likely related in some way but obviously not by birth since Molly was Caucasian.

A simple Google search of Lee Chen was a dead end – almost like his name had been scrubbed from the internet. So, Kate resorted to more clandestine search options. A look at a Canadian criminal database indicated that Chen had been convicted of industrial espionage relating to a Canadian tech company. He had served no jail time but paid a substantial fine. Chen's name popped up on some dark sites, but the details were obscured by the fact that the sites were mostly in Mandarin. The site logos seemed ominous. She made a note to ask her brother about language translation software.

Next Kate searched for information on Hank Gottfried. A conventional website advertised Gottfried's consulting business under the clever name of Gottfried Consulting. Apparently, he specialized in providing assistance to Far East companies trying to do business in Canada and the U.S. The basic business model and Gottfried's experience looked legitimate. Gottfried had no criminal record.

Although the Super Trooper had acquired some information on Max Karelian, Kate was curious to see if there was more. She was especially interested in his association with the delinquent defense contractor, Unified Defense Systems. Kate managed to find several articles from Virginia and Washington D.C. newspapers in March 2005 that described the trial of the four men who had been accused of potential war crimes. Apparently Karelian supervised a team of four men who were charged with providing security for various civilian aid groups. Hostile fire triggered an over-reaction by Karelian's team that resulted in the deaths of numerous non-combatants including women and children. The photos of the event were disturbing. Much to Kate's amazement, the group from Unified Defense Systems was found to be not guilty, their actions apparently justified by the fog of war. Nevertheless, Karelian and his team were fired and excoriated in the local newspapers.

Following the trial, Max Karelian dropped off the radar completely, not surfacing until his appearance at the remote Alaskan mining camp on the west side of Cook Inlet years later. Kate was intrigued by his absence from any kind of records until he applied for a passport shortly before coming to Alaska. What had he been up to? Kate suspected that he had ended up as a mercenary in some foreign struggle, probably traveling under an assumed name and falsified documents.

Next on Kate's list was an attempt to get more information on the mysterious corporate structure of Northwest Base Metals and the shell company, Salish Sea Ventures. Readily available public records provided no information beyond that which had already been uncovered by the state troopers. A deeper dive into less-well-known sources suggested that encrypted messaging had occurred within the companies, but the encryption combined with mostly Mandarin text made it impossible to get much insight.

Since breaking through the wall of secrecy around the corporations was proving difficult, Kate thought that following the money might be more productive. Although obtaining financial records normally required some kind of court order, James had suggested that there were many exceptions and banks were often targets of hackers. Kate had no idea which banks, if any, were involved. What she really needed was access to Lee Chen's computer as a place to start.

After a full day of staring at the lap top screen, Kate was frustrated that she had not uncovered more useful stuff. But, on the other hand, she was learning a lot about sneaky online tricks and was feeling sort of proud of herself.

Chapter Nineteen

"I've got something to show you," Max Karelian said to Travis Chen as he fired up his laptop and inserted a tiny data card into a card reader. A blurry red-tinged image appeared on the computer screen showing a ghostly figure moving across the camp compound.

"Holy shit," said Travis. "When was this?"

"Night before last."

The two men were sequestered in Max's tent, which he occupied alone – apparently one of the perks of being an unfriendly security man. The video recording was from a camouflaged camera hidden in a tree, and the time stamp indicated that the video was from 2:10 a.m. The motion-activated game camera had been a stock item purchased from Cabela's catalog. The small camera was packaged in a waterproof camouflaged case and used infrared illumination during conditions of insufficient visible light.

"We can't see the guy's face, but judging from his tall, gangly build, a good guess might be the hippy-looking guy that was with the trooper when they stopped by last week," Max suggested. "The odd shape of his head suggests he might have been wearing night-vision goggles. Maybe someone who has been professionally trained. We also can't see exactly where he went but at least we know he was moving around near the back of the camp. Was there any disturbance to your metal shed?"

"I didn't notice anything. The door was locked with no sign of a break-in."

"If the guy is that sneaky, he's probably capable of picking a lock."

"I don't know. It's a pretty good lock."

"When you go back there, take a good look around."

"Yeah, I'll check on it tonight. Fuck, I'm going to have to call the boss about this."

†

Bob the Super Trooper sat at the worn gray desk in his tiny office. He was processing some of his never-ending paperwork. He sighed and tilted back in his rickety office chair. On the wall was a ten-year-old calendar featuring bikini-clad blond women in various intimate poses with chainsaws. The Swedish chainsaw manufacturer's promotional calendar was left over from the construction company that occupied the office before he took over. He knew he should remove it but had never gotten around to it. Staring at scantily clad women seemed to improve his concentration.

He was thinking about the murders across the inlet. The investigation was pretty much at a dead end. There was no forensic evidence other than the one bullet found in Jeremy's body. But it was useless unless a gun suddenly appeared – a very unlikely scenario given the remote location of the crime. The persons contacted during the visit to the Northwest Base Metals camp were obvious suspects, but all had reasonable alibis. It was not probable that one of them could have made the seven-mile journey through difficult terrain, killed the geologists, and walked back to camp all in a single night. The security guy, Max Karelian, was the only one who appeared to be in good enough physical condition, but even so it seemed like a stretch. Analysts at trooper headquarters were looking into the Northwest Base Metals company structure and the ownership of the mysterious shell corporation, but the Canadian authorities were not being very cooperative. The break-in at South Peninsula Gold was closer to home, but still there were no clues. In short, he had nothing.

Bob had a feeling that Charlie and the gang were conducting their own investigation. In some ways they had better resources than he did and were less hobbled by pesky legalities. He just hoped that they could come up with something without doing anything so illegal that he would have to arrest them.

As he was contemplating the frustrating state of affairs, the outer door to his office opened and Bryce Cameron, the apparently clueless investor, entered his inner sanctum.

"What can I do for you, Mr. Cameron?"

"Good morning. I was on my way to Anchorage but decided to fly into Homer first and see how your investigation was going."

"The investigation is proceeding. Unfortunately, I can't really say any more than that."

"OK. I also wanted to let you know that my recent attempts to contact any of the project principals are being stonewalled, so I'm going nuts with worry. I have an appointment with a lawyer in Anchorage to see what recourse I might have to recover some money or at least get some answers."

"Well, that's interesting. I certainly wish you luck. If you find out anything new that might help us with our investigation, I would appreciate a heads-up. Have you heard any names mentioned in your contacts with the Northwest Metals people that you forgot to tell us before? Any other information that might be helpful?"

"No other names, but I do remember that Hank Gottfried received a call during my first meeting with them. He left the room, but I could hear that the conversation was in Chinese."

"Thanks. That may be helpful," Bob said dryly as his eyes scanned

Cameron's disheveled face and wrinkled clothes. "Have a safe trip to Anchorage and watch yourself." Cameron nodded his good-bye and Bob's eyes trailed after him as he exited. The trooper leaned back in his chair and massaged his non-existent beard. He pondered whether the spiraling investor could be a viable suspect — and was snooping around for more reasons than he had mentioned. On the one hand, his cluelessness might just be an act, but, on the other hand, he did not seem like the kind of guy that would sneak into a remote camp and kill people. He definitely had motive to optimize the success of the mine, since his financial future depended on it.

Bob called Charlie and arranged to meet at Charlie's boat the following morning at nine.

†

"Good evening, Uncle," said Travis Chen while sitting at the little bench in the mystery metal building. "I have some disturbing news. Two nights ago, one of our hidden video cameras caught someone sneaking around in the back of the camp near my little building. We don't know whether he discovered anything useful, but Max thinks he might have been professionally trained because of the way he moved and because of the probable use of night-vision equipment."

"Did he get into the building?"

"I don't know. There was no sign of forced entry and nothing was disturbed inside. If he did get in, he picked the lock and was careful once he was inside."

"What did he look like?"

"We couldn't see his face because of the blurry image and night-vision goggles, but he was tall and gangly. Max suspects that it was the long-haired hippy guy that came along with the trooper during their visit. Whoever it was hiked all the way through the woods to get there – something only a slightly crazy person would have done. We would've heard a chopper if it had dropped him off, so that seems unlikely."

"OK, we need to take some kind of action to deal with this threat. Do we know the name of this person?"

"Yeah. Max wrote down the names of the visitors. His name may be Johann Bachman. His friends called him JB. As far as I know, he lives in Homer."

"I'll get someone to get more details and look into his past. Then I'll figure out what we need to do."

†

Much later that night, JB used the satphone to query his illicit recording device in the mystery building. Over the satphone's speaker he could hear a door open and close, the beeping of a phone number pad, and eventually a voice. "Holy cow. It really works," JB said to himself with glee. After listening for a few minutes his mood changed. "Oh, crap."

Chapter Twenty

At six a.m. the following day, Charlie emerged sleepily from his teak-lined master suite in the former fish hold of the Shearwater. Kate was still snuggled under the down comforter snoring softly. The tide was low, exposing the fragrant intertidal flats. The sun, breaking over the ridge to the northeast, made the sky pink and glinted off the glaciers on the south side of the bay. Activity in the harbor was beginning to pick up as the halibut charters prepared their boats for the onslaught of day-trippers.

Charlie entered the main cabin, started a pot of coffee, and sat down to think about how to handle the meeting with Bob. He glanced at the *Otterly Ridiculous* next door and noticed some movement, which was very unusual, given JB's habit of sleeping late. Soon JB emerged wearing shorts and a hoody. He was barefoot and looked characteristically disheveled. He was accompanied by Beverly, who looked great as usual. Seeing that Charlie was up, JB and Beverly came aboard the Shearwater, sat down, and helped themselves to coffee. Without a word, JB set his phone on the table, and pushed the play button on the recording function. Beverly stood beside him. The one-sided conversation JB had recorded a few hours earlier played.

"Oh, shit," Charlie said. "We've stepped into a hornet's nest again."

"Yeah. I guess we should assume the worst since two people have already been killed for no real good reason."

"We're going to have to let Bob know that you may be in danger. It will probably take a while for the Northwest Base Metals thugs to investigate your whereabouts and your daily routine, which, I might add, mostly consists of hanging out here with us," Charlie replied. "Homer is a small town and most people know us. If we leave word in the right places we may be able to a get a line on who is investigating. They won't find much on social media or the internet, so they will have to come to town."

"How do we keep getting ourselves into these situations?" asked Beverly. "Where's Kate?"

Coincidentally Kate emerged from the former fish hold still wearing flannel pajamas printed all over with little hippos.

"Wow, that's really sexy," remarked JB.

"Shut up," Kate said through a yawn. "Are we having a meeting?"

"JB has some alarming new information," Charlie said as he played the recording again.

"Oh, crap," mumbled Kate. "Does anybody see a similarity to the situation that we were in last year? Why did I ever get involved with you guys?"

"I was thinking the same thing. I'd chalk the guys' behavior up to testosterone except that we gals have been sort of involved too," Beverly remarked as she reached for her whistling phone. "That was a text from my DEA analyst. She was unable to get any information on the landline number on the phone from the mystery building."

"As it turns out, I have already identified the man behind the phone," said Kate. "His name is Lee Chen and he has an office in Vancouver's Chinatown. While you guys have been out playing I have been actually accomplishing something thanks to my new computer skills and a little help from my brother."

"Wow. What else have you discovered?" asked Beverly.

Kate described the results of her investigations with emphasis on the questionable character of Max Karelian and Lee Chen, as well as on corporate ties to the Chinese underworld. "It occurred to me that following the money might be helpful in trying to figure out exactly what is going on, but I would need to get into Lee Chen's computer or else find out which banks are involved. Maybe Beverly and I can combine forces to get a better handle on who is paying the bills," added Kate.

"I guess we can assume that the Chen family is somehow involved in all this," said Charlie. "The guy JB observed talking to Max Karelian at the camp may be the same as the guy named Travis that the cook told us about. The mystery man obviously has some relationship with Molly Chen since he called her multiple times. So, maybe his last name is also Chen. Possibly Molly's husband. Travis, or whatever his name is, must be related to Lee Chen, maybe son, nephew, or cousin."

"So, what do we do with all this information," asked Beverly. "Law enforcement can't take any action until they have some legally obtained evidence to act on. And what do we tell the trooper?"

"I think we should play the tape for Bob. He'll be flustered, but I think he'll be willing to help by using his contacts to try and detect whether anyone is asking about me," JB said. "Meanwhile, I can be bait. If someone attacks me, it will provide some actionable information allowing Bob to pursue things."

"That's a swell idea," Beverly retorted with a scowl. "First of all, it assumes that you will still be alive with a story to tell. Secondly, I hadn't planned on spending my vacation playing body guard for you."

"Unfortunately, whatever is going to happen is already in motion whether we tell Bob or not," added Charlie.

Coincidentally, at the mention of his name, Bob stepped aboard, accompanied by significant rocking of the boat. Somewhat surprised at seeing Beverly, they greeted each other and shook hands. "Are you here because of dead bodies again?" asked Bob.

"Believe it or not, I've been planning this move for months, but seem to have stepped into it again," Beverly grumbled.

Charlie handed a mug of coffee to the Super Trooper. "We've got some information for you that you're probably not going to like."

"I can't wait." Though not surprised, Bob was still uneasy.

JB gave Bob a sheepish smile and played the recording once again.

"Where the hell did you get that?" asked Bob with a look of frustration. "I'm guessing that I really don't want to know."

"That's probably best for now, but the important thing is that JB may be a target for bad stuff, and I may be a target as well. We were hoping that you could put out some feelers with your contacts to let you know if anyone is asking around town for us. They'll have to do some investigating to find us," said Charlie.

"What else don't I want to know?"

"We're pretty certain that Northwest Metals is behind the murders, but it doesn't look like the whole crew is involved," Charlie continued. "The security guy, Max Karelian, and one of the drillers – the guy heard on the tape – may be the only suspects from the camp. Do you remember when we talked to the cook at their site? She mentioned the name Travis as someone who could be involved in extracurricular activities. A couple other items of interest – members of a family named Chen in Vancouver are probable suspects. It is very likely, if the camp were somehow searched right now, incriminating evidence from the murder scene would be found."

"That's just great, you guys," Bob muttered as he set his coffee down. "What am I supposed to do with this information?"

"We understand that you can't take action based on what we have told you, let alone get a search warrant, but, if JB gets attacked and the perpetrator is captured, I assume that would provide reasonable cause. So there is a bright side, assuming JB survives, of course," added Charlie.

"I'm looking forward to it," said JB.

"Jesus Christ," said Beverly as she rolled her eyes.

"Even though this is a really stupid plan and I'm sure you guys have broken many laws, I guess I don't have much choice but to ignore your transgressions. My investigation is pretty much going nowhere," Bob said. "I'll ask some folks around town to keep an eye open for anyone asking about the two mooseketeers. Please keep me in the loop and give me a call if you need backup."

"Thanks, Bob. We appreciate it," Charlie replied.

"I hope I won't regret this," said the Super Trooper, accompanied by more rocking as he stepped off the boat.

"Well, that was fun," said Kate. "By the way Janine confirmed that the radiation meter that JB photographed in the mystery building was definitely the same one that she rented. The rental company only has one of those things and that was it."

"I guess we should alert the 'spit rats' and harbor businesses to also be on the lookout for persons inquiring about JB," said Beverly. During the summer fish processing season many temporary workers historically descended on the Homer Spit to work long hours in the processing plants. Some of these workers camped on the spit, creating a sort of unique culture, becoming known as spit rats. In recent years, economic development, government regulation, and increased crowding from tourists have partially eliminated the spit rat community.

"Also, we should ask Mike at Kachemak Choppers to watch for Hughes 500 helicopters that may have originated from the NBM camp, especially if they drop someone off," added Charlie. "Meanwhile, I suggest we go fishing since it is a beautiful day."

"I second the motion," Beverly said.

†

After leaving the harbor, Bob pulled up to Gertie's Tavern, known as the headquarters for many of Homer's sleaziest pub patrons. It was still mid-morning and the bar had not opened for the day. The front door was unlocked, as Bob knew it would be, and behind the bar was its namesake elbow deep in the sink and washing dishes. Gertie was a large woman in her fifties with bleached blond hair and a face that may have been quite attractive at an earlier time. But Gertie's most impressive feature was her very large front and amazing cleavage, amply displayed by a low-cut peasant blouse. Even more amazing was the colorful tattoo of an iguana that started on the side of her neck and plunged into the aforementioned cleavage. The legend of Gertie's frontispiece had spread far and wide and was a primary marketing draw for her establishment.

While Gertie was a crude and bawdy woman, she was basically a good person and had helped the troopers on various occasions as long as it did not hurt her business. In the past year she had kindly established a bar fund to help with the costs of a drug rehab program for Bob's current girlfriend.

"How can I help out the troopers this morning?" asked Gertie.

"There's a possibility that some unpleasant people may be trying to get information on JB and Charlie Skyler. I'd appreciate it if you could let me know if anybody like that comes in here. It would be best if you don't give away any information about their locations."

"How did those guys manage to get in the shit again? Does this have anything to do with the geologists who were killed across the inlet?"

"Maybe."

"OK. I'll keep my ears open, and I'll ask some of my more trustworthy regulars to do the same."

"Thanks, Gertie."

†

The Shearwater rolled lazily on the small swells offshore from the town of English Bay, just outside the entrance to Kachemak Bay on the south side. The Shearwater rocked gently, pulling on its anchor twenty fathoms below. Winds were mostly calm and the sky was mostly clear. The usual light haze over the water gave the world a suffused appearance. The view west and south over Lower Cook Inlet included three volcanic peaks, each of which was topped by a graceful lenticular cloud. Sea otters could be seen in the kelp beds closer to shore doing their otter thing − diving to the bottom and returning to the surface with a crab or a sea urchin. The sound of cracking shells could be heard from the Shearwater as the otters consumed their prey.

Charlie, Kate, and Beverly, holding stiff, heavy fishing rods, stood side-by-side along the gunnel on the starboard side. Eighty-pound-test line ran from each rod down to the sea floor where sixteen-ounce lead balls bounced along the bottom. Dangling from each weight was a wire leader with a chunk of herring hooked at the end. JB lounged on a pile of boat cushions and watched the action or lack thereof. JB claimed that he was ethically opposed to killing fish, although he apparently wasn't ethically opposed to eating them. The gang was taking a break from considerations of dead bodies because, after all, it was supposed to be Beverly's vacation. Fishing was slow, as halibut fishing tends to be. The four friends were still enjoying the day and each other's company.

"So, Beverly. What are your plans?" asked Kate. "Are you going to become a boat bum with JB?"

"Frankly the boat bum idea doesn't appeal to me very much. I can't picture myself spending the rest of my life in JB's cave. A small house seems like a much better idea. But I have officially given notice to the Bureau and I'm thinking of becoming a private investigator. That would fit well with my skill set, but I have no idea whether this area could support a PI. What do you guys think?"

"I can attest to the fact that there is a lot of marital infidelity in Homer," remarked JB.

"I would hope that a PI would have things to do other than take pictures of wayward spouses," said Beverly.

"If you consider the whole state as your marketing area it might work out," Charlie said.

JB frowned at Beverly. "I can't believe you would consider abandoning the Otterly Ridiculous."

"Come on, JB," Kate laughed. "There's two feet of clearance above your bed. I would think that would interfere with essential activities. But seriously, Beverly, a PI business seems like a great idea."

"Maybe you and Kate could work together. For example, following the money could come in handy in figuring out where the funds are coming from at Northwest Base Metals," suggested Charlie.

"Actually, the thought of combining forces had already occurred to me. Kate could work for me as a paradetective, if there is such a thing. So, are you guys going to be my first clients?" quipped Beverly.

"Maybe we can pay you in halibut," said Charlie.

"At the rate we're catching them, it could take several decades."

Chapter Twenty-One

The following Sunday morning, Kate woke up determined to see if she could get more information on the source of money supporting the NBM project. The day before, she had sent a bogus email to Lee Chen's computer using the email address gleaned from the smart satellite phone in the mystery building. Kate's brother had sent her his personal attack email, which included a spyware attachment along with software for her computer that would allow her to remotely control other computers. Theoretically, these items would allow Kate to take over the infected computer and search its contents. The plan would only work if Chen opened the attachment containing the spyware; consequently, Kate had customized the title to make it tempting to him by referencing an article on deteriorating Chinese−American relations due to industrial espionage.

Kate was very surprised to find when she opened the remote control software on her computer that Lee Chen had actually opened the attachment, and she now had virtual access to his computer. She started by looking at the file structure and found that some of the files were encrypted and some were not. The encrypted files seemed to mostly concern the technical details of the Alaska mine project, while other files dealing with more mundane business details were mostly readable, but boring and not very useful.

Next, she looked at Chen's browser history to see what internet sites he had accessed recently. Among them was a website for the Asian-American Bank, presumably a financial institution that catered to Asian expats and businessmen. The site had been visited three times in the previous week. Lee Chen's account information was, of course, password protected. But just knowing the bank's name was a step in the right direction. She tried a couple of obvious passwords but, unsurprisingly, was not successful in opening Chen's account. Another option would be hacking directly into the bank's computer system, but such an activity was beyond her current capability, not to mention totally illegal. It was time to get help.

Kate left her cozy spot on the settee in the Shearwater's cabin and walked the twenty feet to the *Otterly Ridiculous*. It was already late morning, and she hoped that she would not be disturbing JB and Beverly too much. Considering how often JB had interrupted her and Charlie, Kate did not feel too guilty about her unannounced visit. Amazingly, they were up and about. The little sailboat cabin smelled strongly of bacon, which was apparently a staple food for the couple.

"What can we do for the beautiful Kate this morning?" asked JB.

"I need your help to engage in more illegal activities," replied Kate. "I managed to gain access to Lee Chen's computer and discovered the name of the bank in Vancouver that he has been using. Unfortunately, I don't have the capability to hack into the bank's computer system. I was hoping that Beverly's colleague at the DEA might be able to help access Chen's account information."

Beverly looked skeptical. "It's true that the DEA has ways of tracking money through the international banking system, but asking Tammy to embark on an off-the-books search could cause her to get into serious trouble within the DEA, not to mention other law enforcement authorities. But, since it's Sunday, Tammy is probably at home. She is a single nerd with a nonexistent social life, so she may be interested in some challenging hacking. I can give her a call right now. I need to touch base with her anyway."

"That would be great."

Beverly called Tammy, who answered immediately. They spent some time catching up on gossip from Beverly's former workplace.

"OK. So what is the real reason for this call?" asked Tammy.

"We were wondering whether you could access Lee Chen's bank account at the Asian-American Bank in Vancouver."

"Is that all? How did you find out what bank he was using?"

"Kate used her new hacking skills to access his computer's browsing history. But that was as far as she could get."

"Wow, you guys are getting good at operating on the edge of legality. I guess there's no reason why I shouldn't contribute to your nefarious activities. Plus, my Sunday afternoon was looking like another Netflix binge marathon. Illegal hacking sounds like a lot more fun. Bank security systems are usually pretty good, but I think my bag of tricks is up to the task."

"That would be great," said Beverly. "We're most interested in the country of origin for money coming into his account or accounts. He may have both a personal account and a business account under the name of Northwest Base Metals Consortium or Salish Sea Ventures."

"OK. I'll see what I can do. I'll give you a call as soon as I find anything useful," added Tammy as she fired up her laptop.

†

Twenty years earlier, when Beverly's colleague, Tammy Vanderhyde, had been a freshman in college, she and some friends had been caught accessing the internal network of a chemical company. The hackers had justified their actions by asserting their belief that the company was a danger to the environment. During the early days of the information revolution in the latter part of the twentieth century, increases in international terrorism and drug trafficking greatly increased the demand for persons skilled in navigating the complex world of cyber sleuthing. Some of the most knowledgeable hackers were young persons who played with computers as a hobby and experimented with illegal hacking because it was fun and represented a form of teenage rebellion. The shortage of people skilled in cyber security forced some institutions and regulatory agencies to hire such persons to help defend against illegal attacks, design secure systems, and access the computer systems of persons and entities that wished to do harm to the United States.

Tammy was one of those persons. As part of a plea deal to avoid jail time, Tammy had agreed to work for the Drug Enforcement Agency as a cyber analyst. After a period of probation, she had become a valuable employee and was appreciative of the legitimate employment. But her cyber excursions for the DEA lacked the excitement and challenge of her earlier activities. So here she was again, engaged in unauthorized hacking.

Using the tools available to her, Tammy had little trouble accessing the account records for customers of the Asian-American Bank. She found that Lee Chen had four accounts for which he was the signatory: personal checking and savings accounts, a business account under the name Northwest Base Metals Consortium, and a business account under the name Salish Sea Ventures. The personal accounts seemed pretty innocuous, with no outwardly suspicious transactions. However, the Salish Sea account record showed large sums of money, up to two hundred thousand dollars per deposit, arriving from unnamed sources on a monthly basis.

Although the senders remained anonymous, Tammy easily tracked down the routing numbers associated with the deposits and determined that they came from two different banks in Beijing. The Vancouver records also showed that funds were periodically transferred from Salish Sea to NBM, presumably to provide funding for the Alaska mine project. Additional transfers went directly from Salish Sea to Lee Chen, possibly payment for services. Tammy ran into a brick wall when she tried to determine which Chinese entity was the ultimate source of money flowing from China to Chen's control in Vancouver.

"So I found out some new stuff," said Tammy during her call later that evening to Beverly. "The funding for your mystery mine definitely comes from China. Funds were sent from an unnamed source to Salish Sea Ventures, and from there to an NBM account as needed for the mine. Lee Chen controls all of the money on the Canadian end. I have no idea who controls the money on the other end, and I suspect that trying to find out would be difficult, if not impossible."

"Wow. That's great," said Beverly. "You need to drink a glass of wine and go to bed. Thanks for your help."

"You guys be careful up there," said Tammy. "Meanwhile, I'll see if I can find out anything else on the mysterious Mr. Chen."

Chapter Twenty-Two

A black Jet Ranger helicopter with a swooshy white design on the side landed in the general aviation area of the Homer airport. A slender man of average height and Asian features climbed out with a duffel bag and proceeded to the rental car counter in the main terminal. He rented a car under the name Michael Yanagawa and proceeded to explore the town and harbor to get a feel for the general area. Prior to coming to Homer he had researched the name Johann Bachman but found nothing on social media and only a little on the internet. It seemed that Bachman had once been a professor at a California university but was no longer there. There were no hits from the last six years. Even stranger was the fact that Mr. Bachman had apparently not existed before his time at the university. Illegal access to various state and federal data banks turned up no normal records from JB's early life, such as Social Security numbers, driver's licenses, passports, and so forth. Mr. Yanagawa was starting to become concerned that Bachman was not your average citizen.

Starting at one end of the Homer business district, he stopped at various public establishments and asked if anyone knew the whereabouts of Johann Bachman. About halfway down the main street he came upon Gertie's Tavern. It was mid-afternoon and already the bar was busy. The establishment disgusted Yanagawa. The dirty floor was covered with peanut shells, and the place smelled like cigarette smoke, beer, and restroom disinfectant. He would never understand how people could degrade themselves by patronizing such a sleazy place. As he approached the long, beat-up bar he was met by Gertie. At first glance of Gertie's assets, he almost turned around and left from embarrassment. But the job came first, and he inquired about Bachman while averting his eyes. Gertie, sensing his discomfort, played dumb and hoisted her boobs up onto the top of the bar in front of him. Yanagawa's face turned bright red and he quickly retreated in humiliation.

He continued his search until he reached the end of the commercial district but was not able to get any information on the mysterious Johann. His secretary had made a reservation at a local motel, so he proceeded to his room to regroup. He was pretty sure that the horrible lady at the bar knew who Bachman was and that she was intentionally trying to divert his attention by embarrassing him. He was ashamed that her strategy had worked pretty well.

†

Charlie was working on correspondence relating to his ecotour business when his phone began playing Beethoven's Fifth Symphony. On the other end was Mike of Kachemak Choppers calling to inform him that he had seen a black helicopter with a white swooshy design land at the airport. One person carrying a duffel had disembarked and walked to the main terminal. Mike had been too far away to distinguish facial features, but he described the passenger as average height and dressed in dark clothing. Charlie rousted JB from his nap and gave him the news. They had been anticipating that someone from the NBM camp might arrive using one of the smaller camp helicopters, so they were a little surprised that the big corporate machine was involved. Charlie called trooper Bob and asked if he could check with the car rental people to see whether someone arriving by helicopter had rented a car. If so, maybe he could get a name and better description for the new arrival as well as a description of the rental car.

An hour later, Bob called back with two pieces of information. The name on the rental car contract was Michael Yanagawa, a slim, studious-looking man with glasses and strong Asian features. The rental car manager, having spent time in the Far East, thought that, although the name was probably Japanese, the man's features suggested Chinese origin. Additionally, Bob had received a call from Gertie at Gertie's Tavern who said that a timid Asian man had been asking about Johann Bachman. Apparently Gertie had scared him away with her unusual physical attributes.

"This guy doesn't really sound like an assassin," said JB. "He may just be trying to find me."

"One possibility might be for us to find him and ask what he's doing. He already knows you're here somewhere, so if we find him on neutral ground, he still won't know where you live," replied Charlie.

"On the other hand, if he really is an assassin, that could turn out to be a bad idea," JB said.

"Yeah. Maybe we should just let things play out. Try to keep track of the mystery man. Eventually, he's going to get a line on where you hang out. We may know when he leaves Homer, assuming the same helicopter picks him up."

"The Harbor Master will let us know if he asks about me at the harbor office. It's against their policy to give out live-aboard locations anyway," added JB.

"If Mr. Yanagawa is simply an investigator, we can probably assume that he will feed information to others in the organization, so we should be ready for anything."

†

After a miserable night thanks to noisy, lustful neighbors and a lumpy bed of questionable provenance, Michael Yanagawa continued his inquiries. He knew that boats were probably involved in accessing the South Peninsula Gold claim area. Therefore, he concentrated his inquiries in that direction. He finally got lucky when he questioned a man coming out of a marine supply store. The friendly fisherman told him that Johann lived on a boat somewhere in the harbor. He also told him that most people knew Johann only as JB.

Parking his SUV in one of harbor parking lots, Yanagawa bought an espresso and sat on a bench on the boardwalk above the harbor. Max Karelian had provided a description of JB which, fortunately, was pretty distinctive. It was a beautiful day, and he settled in for the long haul, thinking that he probably had a pretty good chance of eventually locating a tall, thin person with wild hair. Yanagawa was patient and would stay as long as it took to find his quarry, even if he had to move from vantage point to vantage point. He was fascinated by the fact that the extreme tides in Cook Inlet caused the floating docks to rise and fall, changing his perspective on the docks. Most of the time Yanagawa was looking down at the boats, providing a very clear view. The busy Alaska harbor environment was alien to him and quite interesting. He enjoyed watching the range of activities and variety of boats in spite of his personal obsession with neatness and cleanliness, a virtue that most Alaskan boat people seemed to lack.

Yanagawa was especially intrigued by the activity at the FlashFrozen dock where commercial fishing boats were unloading their catch. The tide was low and fish were being hoisted from the holds of the boats twenty feet up to the top of the pile-supported pier. The net-like bags full of halibut were emptied onto sorting tables where the fish began their journey through the processing plant. Michael was especially fond of halibut and his mouth started to water.

He had no luck on the first day of harbor observations. On the second day he established a new observation post farther south along the harbor side. At eleven o'clock he saw a tall, disheveled man accompanied by a petite woman with short hair emerge from a rickety sailboat and walk to the commercial-fishing-style powerboat next door and enter its cabin. Using binoculars, he could see two men and the woman through the cabin window. A few minutes later the trio left the cabin with cups of coffee and sat in chairs on the deck. The second man had a blond beard and stout physique. He was pretty sure these two men were the same ones that had visited the NBM camp with the trooper, per the descriptions given to him. He noted the boat slip locations using the numbered harbor reference points and continued to watch. He thought it was interesting that, although it was the middle of a work day, neither man was working. It was just more evidence of the slovenly Western work ethic.

Yanagawa had been ordered to not only locate the men but also to get some idea of their daily schedules. He continued to watch, breaking to eat and occasionally exercise his legs. At about one o'clock the man called JB and the woman went back to his boat and the other man entered his boat cabin and remained there. At four thirty, a young woman with long brown hair walked past his position above the harbor, proceeded down the ramp to the floating dock area, and entered the powerboat occupied by the bearded guy. Everybody stayed where they were until Yanagawa called it quits at about nine p.m.

Back in his motel room he accessed the motel Wi-Fi and sent an encrypted email to his boss in Vancouver describing what he had found.

†

After JB and Charlie received the description of their probable pursuer and his rental car, they began a systematic watch of the harbor margin. JB was able to observe most of the western side of the harbor through a small porthole in the side of his sailboat cabin without being seen from above. This technique had been established during a similar surveillance two years before. On the day after the report from the rental agency, JB observed an Asian man calmly sitting on a bench above the harbor. He called Charlie and they agreed to emerge from their boats to see what the watcher would do. As it turned out, the watcher just kept watching until nearly dark, then left. It was obvious that he was observing them specifically.

JB and Charlie figured it was especially critical that they try to get a recording that night of any phone conversations from the NBM camp since it could involve discussions of how the NBM folks wanted to deal with the rogue Homeroids.

JB accessed the recorder at about two a.m. As anticipated, the phone in the little mystery building had been quite active. The first call was from Travis to Molly Chen and turned out to be a normal conversation between separated partners. The second call was to someone in authority, maybe Lee Chen. The side of the conversation picked up by the voice recorder was disturbing:

"Good evening, Uncle. What have you heard from your investigator?"
Pause.
"OK, I got that. What do you want us to do?"
Pause.
"Is that really necessary? Seems pretty risky."
Pause.

"Why me? It seems like Max would be a better candidate."

Pause

"I'm not happy about this. How the fuck am I going to make it look like an accident?"

Pause

"Yeah, yeah. Take it easy, Uncle. I'll keep you posted."

JB went back to bed but was unable to sleep. At six a.m. he resumed watch at his porthole observation post. A short time later the Asian man returned to his park bench surveillance above the harbor. At six forty-five, Charlie and Kate emerged from their love nest in the bowels of the Shearwater and started their breakfast routine so that Kate could get to work at eight o'clock. JB and Beverly joined Charlie and Kate, grabbed cups of coffee and sat in their usual places on the settee in the galley.

"I'm guessing from your sleepy appearances that you didn't sleep much last night," remarked Kate.

"Yeah." JB played the recording that he had transferred to his phone.

"Shit," Charlie muttered. "Here we go. At least we know the guy currently watching us is probably not an assassin. We can expect Travis, or whatever his name is, to arrive somehow from the NBM camp and take up the chase. How can we orchestrate things to our advantage? It would be good if we could encourage events to occur away from the harbor."

"Our watcher is sitting up there as we speak. We can probably assume they are trying to get some idea of our daily movements. Maybe if I look like I'm engaged in some kind of predictable daily activity we can lure them into making a move," JB said.

"Oh, great," replied Beverly. "We can set you up for a sniper.

Sounds like a brilliant plan."

"Nothing's going to happen today, or probably tomorrow, since they need time to get here and plan their moves. Plus, I'm betting that they don't want to do anything as obvious as a sniper attack. Bob wouldn't be able to ignore the possible connection with NBM and might request a camp search warrant. It sounds like they're thinking of encouraging some kind of accident," replied JB as he helped himself to some of Charlie's granola. "How about if I pretend to teach a course at the college. I am, after all, a former professor."

"That might work," replied Charlie. "The road to the college is curvy and runs through the forest for about a half mile. Could be a good spot for an accident."

"How would you defend yourself against such an attack?" asked Kate.

"I don't know. I guess we'd have to consider all the various options, such as being run off the road or someone tampering with my car," said JB.

"With the condition your car is in, it might not be necessary to tamper with anything," quipped Beverly.

"This might be a good time for me to leave to get to my fictional eight o'clock class. We can see whether our watcher follows," said JB.

JB returned to the *Otterly Ridiculous* to put on somewhat more respectable clothes and proceeded to his car parked in the harbor lot above his boat. As anticipated, the Asian man followed in his rental. JB continued to the college parking lot, got out of his car, and entered one of the buildings. Charlie and Beverly followed behind the watcher. The Asian man observed JB enter the college building before turning around and backtracking to town where he parked at a motel and was seen entering one of the outside-entry rooms.

Much later in the day JB checked the voice recorder in the mystery

building at the NBM camp. To his surprise, there was no additional
phone traffic.

Chapter Twenty-Three

The next morning the watcher was back at his post, and JB repeated the early morning trip to the college. Again the watcher followed, then came back to the harbor to continue observations. Charlie called the Super Trooper to let him know that there was a good chance that JB would be targeted in some way. Charlie also called Mike, the helicopter pilot, to watch for any Hughes choppers from the NBM camp or any other suspicious aircraft dropping off people at the airport.

Meanwhile, Beverly and Charlie were visiting in the cabin of the Shearwater while Kate was at work and JB was off playing assassination bait. Beverly had been corresponding again with her data analyst, Tammy, back at the Los Angeles DEA office. Another call came in from Tammy as Beverly and Charlie started on their second cup of coffee.

"Hi Tammy. What's up? You're on speaker-phone so my friend Charlie can hear."

"How come whenever you go to Alaska you get involved with some weird shit? I followed up on some of the information that Kate and I turned up. It turns out that this Lee Chen guy is pretty interesting in a creepy sort of way. He has been on the radar of both Canadian authorities and the NSA for quite a while for industrial espionage and a variety of illegal pro-China activities. He has advanced degrees in chemical engineering and minerology and is vested in expanding China's hi-tech profile by any available means. There are rumors that he has ties to both the Chinese central government and Chinese organized crime."

"Why isn't he in jail?" asked Charlie.

"Apparently he keeps himself far enough removed from the action to effectively insulate himself from prosecution, plus crimes like industrial spying are often vague enough to make them hard to prosecute."

"Are there any hints of violence associated with Chen?" asked Beverly.

"None that have been proven, but some of Vancouver's better known Chinese citizens have mysteriously disappeared. Chen was investigated as a possible accomplice in the crimes, but none of the accusations stuck. He is known to surround himself with a thuggish protection detail when moving about town," replied Tammy.

"Anything on Travis Chen?" asked Charlie.

"Nothing nefarious – just some Facebook stuff. He seems like your normal guy with a pretty wife, a young son, and some friends he hangs with. Actual photos of Travis on social media seem to be lacking, which I guess is sort of odd."

†

Mid-morning on the same day a bright blue Hughes 500 helicopter landed at the Kenai airport about sixty-five miles north of Homer. A "normal guy" carrying a large duffle bag disembarked and walked to a car rental booth where he rented a nondescript compact car using falsified documents. Travis Chen was in the middle of some serious self-reflection. His Uncle Lee had been a lifelong benefactor, paying his way through college and graduate school and providing employment. But his current assignment definitely stretched the limits of loyalty. He had somehow, by virtue of his birthright, automatically become part of the Chinese effort to subvert U.S. and Canadian institutions in order to gain Chinese advantage. These activities often involved spying, violence, and association with the Chinese underworld. What he really wanted to do was lead a normal life as a responsible family man in suburban Vancouver. Instead, he was on his way to Homer to orchestrate an "accident." Travis was not a total stranger to the idea of violent pursuits. His uncle's training regimen had included martial arts and weapons use, and family lore contained many dark stories of association with shadowy crime syndicates. However, up until this point he had managed to avoid being personally involved in violence. He was seriously conflicted about the task that lay ahead.

As he drove southward, he thought about the various possibilities of creating a convincing accidental death. His uncle's investigator had, of course, briefed him on the basic lifestyle and habits of Johann Bachman. Other than exploding boats and car wrecks he was at a loss for ideas. Blatant assassination was out of the question. He could maybe make JB disappear without a trace, but suspicion would still be directed toward NBM. The tendency of Mr. Bachman to hang out at his boat most of the time complicated matters because of the high level of activity in the harbor area. Travis was not a water person, knew little about boats, and definitely was not going to go swimming in the harbor. Whatever action he took needed to occur at a more remote location, which pretty much left a car accident as the only possibility.

When Travis reached Homer, he contacted Michael Yanagawa, who was still on watch. Bachman and his friend Skyler were apparently still on their boats. He then drove around for about two hours familiarizing himself with the area, including a special emphasis on the road to the college. Bachman's daily trip to the college seemed to be the only time when he was reliably away from populated areas. He noted that one of the sharpest curves on the road had a steep drop on its outside edge which made it a logical place to stage a serious one-car accident. There was a flimsy guardrail at road edge, but Travis was pretty sure that it would not stop a car going at normal speeds. Reporting from Yanagawa indicated that Bachman drove fast in an older Jeep Wrangler that was not in the greatest shape, facts which probably aided his mission. Old Jeeps were not known for their safety or highway stability.

He drove around the curve several times from both directions and came up with a plan of sorts. He needed to make the car lose control at just the right time so that the driver would not have a chance to stop or correct his direction. How the heck was he going to do that? A tack strip, similar to what policemen used, would probably do the job but would be a little conspicuous. Nails or other sharp objects on the road might work but would be unreliable considering modern tires were more resistant to blowouts. Shooting a tire as the car rounded the corner was a possibility, but it would be a tricky shot and might not cause a total loss of control. A brake failure at just the right time might work, but how could that be accomplished? One idea that had been in the back of his mind since before he left the camp was the use of a remotely detonated small explosive charge to sever a brake line. He had brought with him from the camp two common elements of a mining operation: a short length of blasting cord and a radio-activated detonator. He could hide in the woods and activate the device as Bachman approached the curve. Of course, he would have to install the device without being detected. But this seemed like the best option. Travis returned to his cheap motel room to meditate and prepare.

†

After JB returned from his bogus college class, he and Beverly retired to the Otterly Ridiculous to relax. On the Shearwater, Charlie was going through emails for his tour business. Every once in a while, the top of the mast on JB's boat jiggled. Charlie was trying not to think too hard about what that might mean when his phone rang.

"Hey, Mike. What's up?"

"You asked me to look out for a blue Hughes chopper. None have landed here, but I was talking to a pilot friend in Kenai about other stuff, and he mentioned that he had seen a blue machine that he did not recognize and asked if I knew where it was from. Apparently one guy got off and went into the terminal. The chopper left immediately. So, maybe this is what you've been waiting for," said Mike.

"Wow. Thanks, Mike. I owe you one," replied Charlie.

"I don't know what you're into, Charlie, but be careful," said Mike as he signed off.

Charlie called JB.

"This better be important," growled JB.

"It is. Can you guys get yourselves together and come over?"

"Whatever do you mean by that? OK, we'll be there in a minute."

JB and Beverly found Charlie sitting at the galley table surrounded by piles of business paperwork. Charlie explained about the call from Mike of Kachemak Choppers.

"I guess we need a plan," said Beverly.

"OK, let's think about this," said Charlie. "Assuming the worst — that the guy who got off the chopper means to do us harm — then we know he is already here. Presumably he's planning his next move. The ways in which he could dispose of JB and maybe myself without incriminating anybody are limited. He could probably stage a boat explosion, but that seems pretty risky. Or he could stage a car accident which seems a little more likely. We should probably guard against both."

"It seems like we've been here before," said Beverly referring to previous events when a psychopath tried to blow up Charlie's boat with him in it. "I feel like the car accident is more likely, especially since we've provided the opportunity with JB making predictable daily trips to the college."

"The road to the college has some nasty curves that are tailor-made for fatalities," added JB. "I've been planning my own demise on every trip. I even know where it will occur. One of the sharpest curves is above a two-hundred-foot drop."

"The way you drive, the bad guys can just let nature take its course," said Beverly. "But, seriously, how could an accident be encouraged to occur at the optimal moment?"

"Blowouts or brake failure come to mind. But the timing would be tricky," said Charlie. "Or the driver could be incapacitated, and the accident set up with the driver in the driver's seat and the car aimed to go off the road at the right location. But knocking out JB without murdering him first would be difficult to say the least and would leave evidence of foul play. Tampering with the brakes might be the best option. If the brake line is cut before JB starts on his journey there would be a reasonable chance that complete failure could occur when braking hard for the curve, but it would still be pretty unreliable. Loss of brake function would likely be noticed before reaching the curve."

"In any event, we should be on the alert for someone messing with the car tonight," Beverly said. "How about staking out the parking lot just in case? I volunteer, since my main squeeze seems to be the designated bait, plus, I have had lots of practice being bored at stakeouts."

"OK. JB and I can watch the boats. If anything is going to happen it will most likely be between one and three a.m."

"Maybe Kate can keep me company part of the time, but she'll probably need to get some sleep eventually," added Beverly. "What do we do if we catch someone in the act of tampering – encounter them immediately or try to catch them later?"

"I think we try to let things play out. None of us has law enforcement authority except Beverly, and she's not here on assignment. If we get some hard evidence then we can call Bob and work with him to follow up on an arrest," replied Charlie. "Do we have a camera that can take pictures in dim light without flashing?"

"My agency phone is set up to do just that," Beverly said with a proud nod.

Chapter Twenty-Four

At just after one o'clock in the morning, Travis got off his bunk, dressed in dark clothing, and headed for the harbor. Earlier that evening he had scoped out the harbor parking lots, memorized the location of JB's Jeep, and planned an inconspicuous avenue of approach. The harbor proper was partly illuminated all night with large lights, but the parking lots were mostly in shadows. He left his car two lots north of the lot containing the Jeep and approached in the shadows. The night was calm, and surface fog, rising from the cool sea water, was creating a mystical effect and providing additional cover. The harbor lights were all surrounded by rainbow-like halos. Not a soul was in sight. The smell of the sea and the tide flats was extremely strong.

His explosive apparatus was all assembled and he had practiced placement in his motel room. As soon as he got to the Jeep he flopped onto the ground and slithered under the vehicle. The high clearance of the 4x4 made it easy to find the brake line, even without light. The blasting cord was wrapped around the line, and the detonating mechanism was magnetically attached to the frame above it. Thirty seconds later he emerged from under the Jeep and retraced his steps. Piece of cake.

†

Beverly was positioned between two stacks of crab pots with a clear view of JB's car. She was essentially invisible because of the harsh shadows and her black Ninja outfit. As a DEA agent she had spent many nights on surveillance duty and had developed various strategies for remaining sane. She always brought padding so she could be reasonably comfortable. In her pack were a dozen Twinkies. As a reward for surviving the mind-numbing boredom, she consumed one every thirty minutes.

She was on her fifth Twinkie when she saw a dark figure approach the Jeep and crawl under. It all happened very fast, but she was able to get the camera positioned to catch the saboteur when he emerged. She managed to get two shots as he left the Jeep, including a partial view of his face dimly illuminated by the harbor lights. Still in the shadows, Beverly stood up and observed the intruder jogging to a subcompact sedan.

After waiting a few minutes, Beverly went to the Jeep and crawled underneath. With a small flashlight she was immediately able to spot the explosive device. After photographing it in place, she carefully removed the device while wearing surgical gloves, placed it in a Ziploc bag, and ran to Charlie's boat where she assumed that either Charlie or JB would still be awake.

"I think we hit pay dirt," Beverly said as she plopped the explosive onto the dinette table and explained where it came from. Explosives expertise just happened to be one of JB's many hidden talents, and he immediately disconnected the detonator from the blasting cord.

"OK. It's harmless now. This is a common commercial arrangement where the detonator is activated by a specific radio signal. Presumably, our friend will be sitting in the woods near the most hairiest curve waiting for me to come by in the morning," said JB.

"We need to call Bob right away so that he can take charge of trying to apprehend our assassin, and we've only got a few hours to get set up," suggested Charlie as he dialed the Super Trooper's private mobile phone.

A sleepy voice answered. "This better be important."

Charlie explained the situation and they agreed that Charlie, Beverly, and Trooper Bob would meet just before sunrise at an out-of-sight location a half mile from the most dangerous curve on the road to the college. JB, being the designated bait, would stay back until time for his morning commute. Kate was assigned the job of communications coordinator, and texting by mobile phone was the primary communication mode.

Charlie, Beverly, and Bob reached the rendezvous point at about four a.m. Bob and Beverly hiked through the forest parallel to the roadway on the side away from the gully. They spaced themselves about thirty yards apart, with Beverly deeper in the woods. Charlie, being the only unarmed member of the team, walked through the woods on the other side of the road on the edge of the gully. The plan was for JB to drive through the critical zone then pull over and join the hunt approaching from the other end.

†

Travis got up with the sun at about four thirty, dressed in dark clothing, filled a pack with essentials including a radio transmitter, and strapped on a shoulder holster with a 9 mm Glock. He drove to a side road that he had identified the day before along the college road, parked out of sight, and began hiking. He reached his position in the dense alders at the top of the road cut on the opposite side of the road from the steep gully. He had good visibility of the approach from town. All he had to do now was wait. Travis was more or less operating on autopilot. Every once in a while, reality would intrude on his consciousness, and he would wonder what the heck he was doing there.

He saw JB's Jeep approaching right on time at seven forty-five – he was going fast as usual. The transmitter was on and ready to go. Everything was working out perfectly. Travis pushed the button. And nothing happened. JB braked smoothly, rounded the curve, and proceeded on his way. *What the fuck?*

†

Beverly, Bob and Charlie timed their approach to the attack zone to coincide with the time when JB would pass by on his way to the college. Bob was the first to see Travis hiding in the bushes just as JB's Jeep passed by on the road below. A few seconds after the failed brake malfunction, Travis heard the approaching trooper and quickly realized what was happening. He drew his gun and fired a quick shot in Bob's direction before running deeper into the woods. He passed within twenty yards of Beverly, who yelled for him to stop or she would shoot. He kept running but turned back toward the road. Beverly could not get a clear shot because of the trees. Plus, she knew that JB could be approaching her rapidly moving target from the opposite direction.

"JB, he's coming your way!" yelled Beverly with no real idea whether JB was close enough to hear.

"I can hear him!" JB yelled back. "He's headed back into the woods. I can track him."

"Go for it. We're right behind you," bellowed Bob. He was hoping that all the chatter would encourage the bad guy to give up. But Travis had other ideas.

JB was very good at tracking fleeing suspects. He had been trained for just such a cat-and-mouse game in his previous life. He knew that the pursued had an advantage since they could select a location to defend and ambush the pursuer. The pursuer, by definition, had to keep looking. So, JB slowed his pursuit and adjusted his mind-set to focus on sensory input. At first, he was able to hear Travis moving through the forest and was able to pick up the trail of damp impressions and broken twigs. But then all became quiet. As he moved slowly along the trail, his peripheral vision sensed movement off to the side. He dove behind a tree as a shot was fired. JB reluctantly removed his little Beretta from his jacket pocket. Surprisingly, the shot was followed by sounds of rapid movement back toward the road. He texted the rest of the team that their quarry was headed in their direction.

Beverly and Bob, alerted by the text, stationed themselves about a hundred feet apart in the underbrush at the edge of the road. Soon Beverly heard movement in the forest. She crouched behind a thick stump. When Travis came into view, she announced her presence and told Travis to drop the gun. He fired a quick shot that hit the stump. He then swerved to the right, running rapidly away from both Beverly and Bob. Travis jumped the road ditch and sprinted up the roadway.

As Beverly ran in pursuit she yelled, "He's probably going for his car."

Beverly was much better equipped for sprinting than the Super Trooper. As she tore ahead with speed and agility, Bob lumbered after her in heavy strides. Travis was a good match for Beverly though. He also was in good shape and was able to gain some ground. As Travis tore ahead, leaving them at least two hundred feet behind, Beverly began to burn out and her pace slowed. The agent in her wanted to keep up, but she was not all that anxious to get too close because of his gun. On the other hand, Travis was too far away for her to get a good shot.

†

Travis thought he had it made. His car was in sight, unlocked and ready to go. He opened the door, pulled the keys from the visor, inserted them in the ignition, turned the key — and the car did not start. Swearing to himself, he jumped from the driver's seat, crouched behind the car, and pulled his gun, ready to defend himself at all costs. The woman and the large cop were approaching but staying behind the shield of the trees. The cop yelled for Travis to drop his gun. He fired twice, but there was too much cover to hit anything except spruce trees. The woman and the cop each shot twice, making holes in his rental car. Two of the bullets passed through both car doors and nearly hit him. Then all went black.

†

"Hold your fire," Charlie yelled as he stood behind Travis's unconscious body with a large stick in his hands. While Charlie had manned his station on the other side of the road, he heard the shots and was able to follow the commotion as it moved up the road. It occurred to him that Travis must have a car parked nearby. He ran down the pavement to a narrow side road, which seemed like a logical place for someone to park, and soon saw the car. Finding that the door was unlocked, he popped the hood, and disconnected the wire leading to the spark plugs. Expecting more gunfire he moved into the forest behind the biggest tree he could find just as Travis was approaching. He watched as Travis was unable to start the car and saw him open the car door and crouch behind. Charlie was alarmed by the volley of gunshots coming from both directions. Fearing that someone would be injured, he took a chance and crept up on Travis during the chaos and whacked him on the head with a heavy tree branch.

Chapter Twenty-Five

At dawn the next morning an Army surplus Huey helicopter took off from the Kachemak Choppers apron and proceeded west across Cook Inlet. The weather was cloudy and somewhat ominous. Inside the machine were Bob the Super Trooper, two additional troopers borrowed from the town of Soldotna, JB, Charley, and Beverly. Bob had initially groused about the mooseketeers being involved in serving the warrant, but he was eventually convinced that the civilians had enough special knowledge of the situation and familiarity with the mine camp that they would be useful during the search.

Immediately after Travis Chen had been captured and placed in the Homer jail, Bob had requested Travis's driver's license and employment records from BC provincial authorities. The license photo and employment records established a solid link with Northwest Base Metals. These records combined with Travis's activities of the preceding day proved to be sufficient for a search warrant. JB felt it was critical that the warrant be served before Travis could make any phone calls that might alert residents of the camp to get rid of any evidence.

The chopper flew just above the trees, came over the last ridge, and immediately dropped down onto the camp landing pad. The camp was just awakening, with a few early risers emerging from the tents and heading to the latrine or the mess hall. JB directed one of the troopers to the mystery building and asked him to stand guard while they served the warrant. Craig Johnson sleepily poked his head out of the door of his quarters, and upon seeing the troopers, swore inwardly and pulled his pants on. Bob approached, showed Johnson the warrant, and asked that all professional staff wait in the headquarters tent without touching anything until the search was over. Beverly was dispatched to watch the headquarters and prevent stuff from disappearing. There were too many people in camp to keep track of, so the workers were allowed to follow their normal breakfast routine.

JB went to Max Karelian's tent but found it empty. Hooks near the front door where outdoor clothing would likely be hung were empty. He did a quick search of Max's belongings but found nothing of interest. No sign of a gun or ammo. A duffle bag under the bed was mostly empty. It seemed likely that Max had already flown the coop.

Moving to the mystery building, JB elected to pick the lock once again rather than try to find keys. Everything looked the same as it had during his first visit. Even the rented radiation meter was still there. He instructed one of the troopers to bag all the contents of the shed and not allow anyone into the building. On top of one of the benches were some field notebooks that he had not seen before. Written on each notebook cover was South Peninsula Gold. Bingo, he thought.

His next stop was the crew tent where Travis had bunked. He asked one of the drillers which bunk belonged to Travis and searched through Travis's belongings, including a duffle under the bed as well as under the mattress. He found a wallet and some identification documents, which he left for later bagging.

Meanwhile Bob and Beverly were trying to deal with a very angry Craig Johnson. The geologist that worked under Craig, Joel Spurgeon, and the young clerical assistant were sitting quietly in the corner.

"The warrant cites conspiracy to commit murder as the justification. What the hell are you talking about? Does this have to do with the murders next door?" asked Craig.

"Not exactly, although that's certainly a consideration," answered Bob. "One of your employees, Travis Chen, was apprehended in Homer while trying to cause an unfortunate accident to occur to Johann Bachman, whom you met on our first visit."

"That's crazy. Travis is visiting his family in Vancouver."

"I'm afraid not. He's currently in the Homer jail," replied Bob.

"Why would Travis want to attack someone?" asked Craig

"We think that Bachman discovered some things about your operation and became a risk to whoever is calling the shots on this project. All of which makes us want to know what your role is in all this. We'd like you to come back to town with us along with Max Karelian," Bob said.

"Am I a suspect in the murders?"

"Let's just say you're a person of interest."

"Karelian's gone," said JB as he entered the headquarters tent. "He must have split as soon as he saw the chopper. I suspect he had a ditch kit all prepared so he could leave quickly. His disappearance is suspicious to say the least."

"But where would he go?" asked Craig Johnson as he shook his head in confusion. "We're in the middle of a wilderness with ocean on one side and mountains on the other. Believe it or not, I'd like to see him caught as much as you guys. I'm rapidly coming to the realization that I've been played throughout this sorry project, and Karelian may be one of the keys to proving that I'm not involved."

"You may well be right," said JB. "I guess he has two choices – lay low and return to camp after we've gone hoping to figure a way out from here, or go cross country to someplace where he can get a ride to civilization. Since he might suspect that we will monitor the camp, my guess is he's going to keep moving. His time in Afghanistan was probably good training for dealing with rugged terrain and general deprivation. There probably isn't much hope tracking him from here. He could be anywhere."

"Meanwhile, what do I do about our exploration operation?" asked Craig.

"We have evidence that the owners of the operation may be involved in a conspiracy that includes the murders," Bob replied. "It is likely that the operation will be shut down. I suggest you ask your young assistant to coordinate a demobilization over a couple of days. I have no idea how you're going to deal with the financial aspects of camp closure. Removal of the structures can probably wait. From what we know so far, your bosses in Vancouver are also going to be in big trouble. We have a lot to talk about when we get back to town."

"I suggest that you wait until we have had a chat before you call Vancouver," Charlie added. "If it is true that you are a more or less innocent bystander, then you may want to get more information before proceeding. And you may want to get a lawyer."

Craig instructed Joel to notify the camp of the plans to shut down and to manage an orderly demobilization. The investigation crew, along with Craig Johnson and various articles of evidence, loaded into the chopper and departed for Homer. One of the troopers was ordered to stay behind and monitor the camp demobilization and watch for the possible return of Max Karelian.

†

Early evening of the same day, Travis sat handcuffed to an immovable metal chair in the room that doubled as the trooper conference and interrogation room. Bob and Beverly sat across from him. Bob guessed it was probably okay if Beverly participated since she was a law enforcement officer, albeit supposedly off duty. Travis had no identification when he was captured. A search of his motel room found a British Columbia driver's license in the name William Gannon and an anonymous mobile phone.

"What the fuck am I doing here?"

"Gee, I don't know, Travis," Beverly scorned. "Maybe the fact that you shot at law enforcement officers has something to do with it."

"My name's not Travis."

"Yes it is," said Bob as he opened a folder with a photocopy of another B.C. driver's license and held it up to Travis's nose.

"How the hell do you know my name?"

"We've been watching you for a while. So, what were you trying to accomplish by lurking along the road?" asked Bob.

"I was just taking a walk in the woods when you guys started chasing me."

"Yeah, right," Bob said as he took three photos out of his folder and placed them in front of Travis. The photos included an image of the explosive device, an image of the device attached to the brake line of a car, and an image of Travis crouching next to the car.

"Holy shit," Travis said. "I think I want to see a lawyer,"

"I think that would be an excellent idea," said Beverly. "I'm sure your bosses at Northwest Base Metals will be anxious to know that your mission was unsuccessful. Also, you may be interested to know that a search warrant was executed a couple of hours ago, so any warning will be too late. I suggest you think about whether you may want to cooperate. Your family in Vancouver may want you back sometime."

Travis turned white and slumped in his chair, a tear streaming across his face.

Chapter Twenty-Six

Max Karelian was up to his knees in a marsh at the side of a river valley, trying to work his way downstream to the coast where travel might be easier. The evening before the cops invaded the camp he had received an uncharacteristic call from Lee Chen, a man whom he had met only once before. Mr. Chen told him that Michael Yanagawa, his spy in Homer, learned that his nephew had been arrested in Homer and that the wheels were coming off the bus. He strongly suggested that Max be prepared to leave quickly if the camp were raided. Max had packed a ditch kit with everything that he would need to survive a prolonged trek through the Alaska wilderness. So here he was – looking for a place to camp at the end of his first day on the run.

Unfortunately, the NBM camp happened to be located in one of the most rugged areas in Alaska, sandwiched between spectacular peaks of the Aleutian Range and the very lonely coast along the west shore of Lower Cook Inlet. Walking was difficult at best. Much of the area on the slopes was covered by alders, which have a bad habit of growing sort of horizontally before reaching for the sun. Consequently, the narrow trunks were a constant tripping hazard. Better footing could be found above the vegetation line – but then it could get cold and windy. The foothills and bogs between the mountains and the coast were crossed by many rivers and streams, some of which were fed by glaciers and, thus, were high and cold during the summer melt. Stream crossings were often hazardous. To top it off, the area had one of the highest concentrations of brown bears in the state. Max had looked at maps before leaving camp and knew that the terrain was difficult. But looking at maps and actually walking cross country were very different things.

The stream course that he was following widened out, and he found some dry ground on a well-drained terrace with birch and aspen trees. He set up camp, pitching his camouflaged tent under a tree to reduce visibility from the air. He was not sure whether he would be pursued immediately. It seemed likely that the authorities would have enough other stuff to do for a while. Nevertheless, he cooked dinner over a backpacking stove to avoid smoke.

After a yummy dinner of freeze-dried spaghetti, Max spread his maps on the ground and marked his location from his GPS. He had walked all day and only covered eight miles. One possible plan was to follow the coast around the south end of the highest mountains and then head north along a stream course toward Lake Clark and the cabin of their investor, Bryce Cameron. He was pretty sure he could scare Cameron into doing whatever he wanted. However, the distance was well over sixty miles, and there were parts that could be totally impassable. But first he needed to call Vancouver and see what was going on. There was a possibility that he could be exfiltrated from somewhere close by if the Vancouver thugs would be willing to arrange it. Using his private satellite phone, he dialed Hank Gottfried.

"Where are you?" answered Gottfried.

"Where do you think I am? I'm in the middle of the fucking Alaska wilderness," Max retorted. "How about getting me out of here?"

"I'm afraid you're on your own. Things are pretty hot here. I shouldn't even be talking to you on the phone. Good luck," Gottfried replied and immediately signed off.

Though Max was pissed, he was not totally surprised by Gottfried's response. The Vancouver guys were not exactly a compassionate group. He began to mentally prepare himself for a prolonged stay in the Alaska outdoors. He was carrying good quality outdoor gear and had about a week's worth of food. He had his pistol, as well as a small folding survival rifle of the kind packed in many aviation survival kits that combined a .22 rifle with a 410 gauge shotgun. He could hunt and fish if necessary to last longer. He had lived on rabbits and squirrels before and he could do it again. There were lots of fish in the streams, and the berries were beginning to ripen. He figured he could easily last for a couple of months, at least until serious cold weather set in – maybe until late September.

Max, feeling confident he could meet the challenge the Alaska wilderness had to offer, crawled into his sleeping bag and went to sleep.

†

The next morning the little conference room at Homer trooper headquarters was packed. Sitting around the table were Charlie, JB, Beverly, Bob the Super Trooper, and Craig Johnson. Johnson had been allowed to spend the night in a motel since he was not officially a suspect, on the condition that he agree to meet the following morning. He had readily agreed.

"OK," said a nervous Craig Johnson. "I have a feeling you guys know more about what was going on at the mine camp than I do. Can you fill me in?"

"There are a couple of things that we know for sure," replied Bob. "We know that Travis Chen tried to orchestrate a plot to harm JB. He was caught in the act. We also found items at your camp in the small metal building that were taken from the camp of the South Peninsula Gold guys, providing a direct link to their murders. We know that your operation drilled on SPG's claim. We know from the satellite phone in the metal building that there were communications from Travis Chen to a Lee Chen in Vancouver. Mr. Chen has been a person of interest to Canadian and U.S. authorities for some time. Trooper investigators are looking into the corporate aspects of all this and are working with the Canadian authorities. We also have a strong suspicion, based on items in the metal building, that Travis was researching the potential for rare earth minerals on the claim by doing some of his own analyses. By the way, Travis has a master's degree in minerology, so he is more than a driller. That about sums things up. So, Craig, what was your understanding of the project?"

"Holy shit," said Craig.

"Before you answer Bob's question," added Beverly. "You might want to consider whether you need a lawyer. You're not an official suspect right now, but you're the only one who can make the decision whether to talk to us or not."

"I understand the lawyer thing, but I think I'll go ahead and tell you what I know, which isn't much. I will admit to complicity in the trespass. I tried to talk the company out of it, but Hank Gottfried applied pressure and I went along. At this point I would be glad to provide South Peninsula Gold with the drill cores if that helps. I had no knowledge of the murders until you guys showed up at the camp. Looking back on things, I recall that the drill crew did see the South Peninsula Gold guys sniffing around the core site on their claim, so we knew that they had discovered the trespass a few days after our crew left.

"I also had no knowledge of Travis's escapades. I thought he was taking time off for family business. The little building has always been a mystery to me, and I have never been inside of it. I thought that Max Karelian was the primary user, maybe for secret communications with Vancouver. I have never heard of Lee Chen, but I suspected the Chinese connection because of other contacts. Over the course of the project, I have become more and more suspicious of the motives of both Karelian and the owner. Based on our core samples, I also was beginning to realize that rare earth minerals might have potential on the site. But my job was to evaluate potential for gold and other base metals, so that is what I concentrated on."

"Evidence at the camp provides a direct link to the murders next door. Do you have any thoughts on who might have been involved?" asked Charlie.

"I guess the obvious conclusion would be either Travis or Karelian. Max would be my first guess. It would have been easier for him to slip away and hike to their camp. He is in good physical condition and has been trained to do that sort of thing. Travis worked a twelve-hour day shift, and it would be a stretch for him to get to the coast, kill people, and get back. As far as I know, he didn't miss any days on the drill crew during that time period. Plus, Karelian is now running, which seems like a tip off," replied Craig.

"From what we know so far, your story seems about right. We'll take your word for it unless we come across some evidence that contradicts it. We have no reason to keep you in custody, but we would appreciate it if you could remain in Homer until things get sorted out," Bob said.

"It might be best to avoid talking to your bosses in Vancouver for now," Charlie added. "I'm sure they are anxious to hear from you, but talking to them could mess with law enforcement efforts and could get you into more trouble as an accessory."

"OK. I'll lay low, but please keep me informed about what is going on. I'd like to get back to my life."

Craig Johnson was dismissed from the meeting. He was feeling bummed out from having been taken advantage of, but at the same time he was relieved. He had started to regret getting involved in the project even before all the drama.

"So, what's happening with Karelian?" asked JB.

"There is an APB out on him, plus we've contacted various lodges and camps across the inlet. Unfortunately, there's not much over there. Mr. Karelian is going to find that area to be a pretty lonely place," answered Bob. "Do you guys have any ideas how we can catch him?"

"It might be a good idea to contact as many float-plane pilots as we can. A lot of flight paths cross the inlet on their way to bear-watching tours or Lake Clark cabins," Charlie said. "I was also thinking that we should try to analyze what Max's options might be. The trooper at the NBM camp hasn't seen any sign of him, so I guess we can assume that he took off cross country. I looked at maps last night and concluded that he would not be able to go north or west because of impassable terrain. He would have to go south at first, then maybe skirt the coast westward. But the question is what would he do then? There are some lodges in the area that he might be able to take advantage of, or, alternatively, he could head north around the end of the Aleutian Range toward Lake Clark. The latter would be a long and difficult trip."

"Given his history, it's my guess that Karelian thinks of himself as a tough guy," asserted JB. "If he has good equipment, he can survive in the bush for a long time at this time of year. My vote is for the long route, in which case he will be walking for several weeks. If he's careful, he can easily stay hidden."

†

After cooling his heels for a night in the Homer jail, Travis was back in the interrogation room a few hours after Craig Johnson had been released from custody. Travis was accompanied by Larry Judd, a lawyer who, at Lee Chen's insistence, had flown to Homer the night before. Of course, they were making him sit there for a while to get him in the proper mood for questioning. He was, in fact, wondering what to do. His Uncle Lee had a very strong pull on him, not to mention that his uncle was scary as hell, but Travis really did not want to spend the rest of his life in jail. He knew they would soon be asking him about his Vancouver connections, whereas traditions of the Chinese underworld demanded total silence. If he said anything, Larry Judd would relay the information to his uncle. On the other hand, information was his only bargaining ammunition. His wife and son were important to him, and they were totally innocent.

In the midst of his dark thoughts, the door burst open, and Bob and Charlie entered.

"So, Travis, is Lee Chen related to you?" asked Bob.

"How the heck do you know about Lee Chen?" answered Travis as his lawyer gave him a very dirty look.

"The satellite phone in the little metal building showed that you called his number many times. We checked on Mr. Chen and found a lot of interesting information," answered Charlie.

The lawyer nodded to Travis and he nervously cleared his throat. "Lee Chen is my uncle."

"And what is your uncle's position on the project?" asked Bob.

The lawyer nodded again. "He is a representative of the owners."

"That's sort of strange since the site manager, Craig Johnson, had never heard of him when we talked earlier today," quipped Charlie.

"Maybe I can help," said Larry Judd. "Northwest Base Metals is owned by a consortium of investors who prefer to remain anonymous. The technical aspects of mineral exploration were relegated to Mr.

Johnson. In addition to his normal duties as a drill foreman, Travis served as a go-between linking the exploration operation to Mr. Chen's oversight."

"What's even stranger is the fact that Travis was using his metallurgical skills to analyze for the presence of rare earth minerals, while Craig Johnson assumed that he was looking for gold," Charlie said.

"The technical aspects of the exploration are proprietary," answered Judd.

"Of course they are," Bob replied. "Not to mention critical to understanding this whole sorry affair. So, Travis, what did you hope to accomplish by causing harm to Johann Bachman?"

"Travis won't be answering any questions relating directly to the charges," interjected Judd.

"Did you murder the two geologists?" asked Bob.

"What? No."

"Shut up, Travis," said his lawyer. "I think we're done here."

†

Early the next morning, Travis left word with the deputy at the jail that he wanted to talk with the investigation team without his lawyer. Bob and Charlie met him in the interrogation room at eight a.m. JB and Beverly chose to remain in bed.

"I think you called this meeting," Bob greeted as he walked into the room.

"Yeah. First of all, I didn't kill the two geologists," Travis blurted. His night in jail had clearly rattled him and he did not look good. "There are half a dozen people who can confirm that I didn't leave camp during the time that they were killed. As you guys have probably already figured out, my uncle has connections to China and, what is worse, Chinese crime syndicates. If I tell you what I know, not only will I be in danger but possibly my family as well. Like the Italian Mafia, they take a very dim view of informers. But I am willing to risk it if you can give me a break on my current charges and promise me and my family safety in some kind of witness protection program."

"I don't know," replied Bob. "Things are obviously complicated by the fact that both Canada and the U.S. are involved, so there would have to be some kind of international coordination and agreement. Let me make some calls. It may take a while, but you're not going anywhere anyway."

"OK," said Travis with a look of relief. "That sounds fair. Meanwhile, can we keep this conversation quiet? I have to play along with my uncle's lawyer for a while until things get settled. Getting killed in jail doesn't sound like a good option."

Chapter Twenty-Seven

Lee Chen was uncharacteristically stressed. He was chain smoking and pacing back and forth in his Chinatown office while trying to parse the information he had received in the previous twelve hours. After Travis Chen's unsuccessful attempt to orchestrate JB's demise, Michael Yanagawa had continued to serve as Lee Chen's eyes and ears in Homer. When he had been unable to reach Travis by phone, Yanagawa assumed the worst and staked out the Homer trooper office to try and figure out what was going on. While waiting he observed Travis being led into the trooper office in handcuffs. He called Lee Chen immediately. Lee dispatched the family lawyer, Larry Judd, to Homer as soon as he knew that Travis was in trouble, or more importantly, that he would be in trouble if Travis said too much.

While waiting for feedback from Judd, Lee first called the NBM mining camp but got no answer at any of the numbers, including the secured line in the mystery building. Then he called his Vancouver assistant, Hank Gottfried, who was also worried about the silence from up north. These facts disturbed Lee Chen greatly. It seemed like things were falling apart. It got worse when Larry Judd reported back that the mining camp had been raided. Judd also suggested he was worried that Travis would eventually confess his involvement and implicate others. Travis had been like a son to Lee, but he was realistic enough to understand that everyone acts to save their butts when under enough pressure. While he was desperate for more information, it seemed pretty clear that the walls were closing in.

Lee's frustration was aggravated by the fact that the technical information was coming together to allow an economic evaluation of the mining prospects for selected rare earth metals. The latest core samples had supported his view that high-value ore existed in the northeast corner of the claim. His latest reports to Beijing outlined a possible approach to the refining processes that would be needed to get the most value out of the minerals at the site, and the high-ranking politicians to whom he answered were anxious to proceed. Being an ambitious and obsessive man, he had described the project in its most optimistic light. The bosses were not going to be happy when they found out that the project was falling apart because of stupid decisions. Backlash was almost certain. Indeed, his life could be in danger.

Lee was a cautious man and he decided that a retreat might be the best course of action for now. But where should he go? Returning to China would save him from Canadian authorities but make him vulnerable to retribution from both politicians and organized crime bosses who had provided much of the project financing. Furthermore, he and his family would become pariahs. He obviously risked arrest if he stayed in Canada. Figuring that arrest was preferable to assassination, he elected to remain in Canada and attempt to elude authorities.

Because of the marginal legality of many of Lee's activities, he had long ago arranged for a safe house that could not be easily traced to him. He called his chief of security and ordered him to pack things for him, his wife, and thirteen-year-old daughter and pick him up at the office as soon as possible. He packed his computers and most valuable files, shredded other incriminating documents, selected a few of his most valuable Chinese antiques, and waited impatiently for his ride.

While waiting, he received a frantic call from Michael Yanagawa in Homer. "You need to get out of there as soon as possible. The cops are on the move, and I think Travis has made a deal with them."

"How do you know Travis is talking?" asked Lee.

"I've been watching the movements of people between the jail and trooper headquarters. Travis was escorted to the trooper offices without Larry Judd. I can only assume that he was dealing on his own. If that is the case, then your involvement has been implicated and cops could be on their way to you as we speak."

Lee's pacing increased in speed and frequency, punctuated by a glance out the front window of his office on each pass to see if his ride was waiting. To Lee's great relief, his entourage arrived about ten minutes later, and soon Lee Chen and his family, along with two body guards, were traveling in their large armored SUV on Highway 99 leading to the Whistler Ski Resort about seventy-five miles from Vancouver. The spectacular scenery of the Canadian Rockies was mostly ignored while Lee tried to figure out what his future might look like. He had never even been to the small chalet in Whistler, so he did not know what to expect. He did not even ski. In fact, he seldom ventured outdoors.

†

As it turned out, Michael Yanagawa's warnings were prescient. Less than an hour after his call to Lee Chen, a team of Vancouver police and RCMP officers arrived at his Chinatown office. Getting no answer when they knocked, they kicked in the beat-up old door and entered the deserted office. They were all surprised by the clean, modern surroundings and classy furnishings. It was obvious that the occupant had left in a hurry, taking some things and leaving other stuff behind. One of the Vancouver officers was Chinese and often helped coordinate busts in Chinatown. Glancing at the antiques and artifacts he said, "Holy shit. Some of this stuff is really valuable. This desk alone is probably worth a hundred thousand dollars. Mr. Chen must have been pretty desperate to leave all this." A search turned up nothing of great interest other than the collection of highly technical mining reference books.

At about the same time, Lee Chen's spacious mansion overlooking the Salish Sea was raided by another team of law enforcement personnel. The home was empty and, again, it looked like family members had quickly packed only essentials before leaving.

"I think we missed these guys by less than an hour," said the team leader. "The bathroom sink and toothbrushes are still wet."

In another area of Vancouver, Hank Gottfried, his wife, and two children were sitting down to dinner in their large suburban home. A loud knock on the door interrupted the tranquil domestic scene. Two policemen and two detectives entered the house, handed a search warrant to Gottfried, and informed him that he was being arrested for fraud and accessory to murder. His home office files and computer were confiscated and he was ushered to jail. It seemed that no one had thought to warn Gottfried of his pending arrest.

†

Meanwhile, the scene back at the Homer Harbor was returning to normal. Charlie, Kate, and JB were lounging on the deck of the Shearwater with beer and chips. Buster the cat was sprawled in a late afternoon sunspot looking like a black throw rug.

"I've been thinking," said Charlie.

"Uh, oh," chuckled Kate.

"It should be possible to recover the drill core samples that were illegally taken from the South Peninsula Gold claim and give them to

Janine so that she has the information if she wants to sell the claim."

"That's a great idea," replied Kate. "How do we do that?"

"Maybe Bryce Cameron can help us," suggested JB as he opened another beer. "Craig Johnson is coordinating the camp closure, but Bryce may still have some influence because of all the money he has sunk into the project. The existing data and core samples must be going somewhere, and maybe the trespass samples can be delivered to Janine."

After the day of lounging, Charlie got Cameron's home number from the Super Trooper and gave it a call. Bryce's wife answered and indicated that he was not home, but that she would give him a message. After hearing the message, she agreed that was the least they could do, given the circumstances. She assured them that Bryce would help even if he did not want to.

Chapter Twenty-Eight

Two Weeks Later

Max Karelian slit open the belly of a female sockeye salmon, sliced open the swollen egg sacks, and added the roe to the last of his freeze-dried camp dinners, which happened to be fettucine alfredo. The end product was a creamy yellow, slightly nauseating mixture with very slippery noodles. He was not crazy about the oily taste of salmon caviar but knew that it was an extremely energy-rich food that would keep him going for a long time. He had caught the salmon by hand in shallow water at the edge of a small headwater stream. After a year in fresh water and three years in the North Pacific, the fish had followed its nose back to the stream where it was born. Max found that the meat of salmon this late in the spawning cycle was pretty bad, but the eggs were in optimum condition. Since the salmon had stopped eating before entering its home stream, several weeks of upstream passage and strenuous spawning-nest construction had burned all of its fat reserves and started digesting muscle. At this point in its life cycle, a female sockeye is primarily a vessel for delivering eggs back to the area where it had started life four years earlier.

After seventeen days of hiking, Max found himself on a high plateau overlooking the south end of Lake Clark. During the previous two weeks he had not seen any evidence of human beings except for an occasional plane in the distance and a few boats far away in

Cook Inlet. But now he was in an area with increased activity. The Lake Clark corridor within Lake Clark National Park was remote but popular in the summer. Float planes overhead were just as common as boats were in the lake. He had even crossed under a transmission line going somewhere. Max began to take more care at not being seen. There were no trees at his current location so he pitched his camouflaged tent between two large boulders and kept a close watch for human activity.

His journey thus far had been extraordinarily difficult. He thought of the prospectors that roamed all over the state at the end of the nineteenth century. Almost no stream was left untouched by gold pans. They were tough guys. Of course, a lot of them never made it back to civilization. The Alaska coast was very different from the dry, rocky terrain of Afghanistan. At least there was no shortage of water. He had crossed dozens of streams and rivers originating from glaciers and mountainside snowmelt. Max's boots were continuously wet, and he felt the beginnings of trench foot. Most of the streams were small and wadeable, but one glacial river was too high and fast to cross. He was forced to hike downstream to where the river divided into several channels before he could find water shallow enough to wade. Most rivers have a web of tributaries at their upper end, but, as Max was discovering, many glacial rivers also have a web of distributaries at their downstream end. The heavy load of sediment carried by these streams apparently settled out downstream as the gradient of the stream decreased, resulting in many shifting channels.

At one spot, he had encountered a glacier that totally blocked his path. The only choice was to go over it in spite of nasty crevasses. He had seen numerous bears far away on the mountainsides along the way but had only had one close encounter. He had walked up on a brown bear feeding on salmon along a stream. The bear did not seem aggressive, but, on the other hand, it had not run away either. He risked a shot in the air from his pistol, and the animal casually wandered off.

The good news was nobody seemed to be chasing him, and wild foods were abundant. The bad news was mosquitos and biting flies were almost unbearable. He had run out of bug dope after the first ten days. Max found himself looking forward to the late evening when he could hide from the bugs inside his tent, giving him a few hours of blessed relief. But, in spite of all the difficulties, Max was feeling remarkably good. He was well nourished and felt physically fit. The countryside was spectacular, and there was no one to boss him around. It was tempting to just stay in the wilderness indefinitely, but he knew that winter conditions made that impossible.

He reviewed his maps while reclining in his sleeping bag prior to calling it a day. When the project first started, he and Hank Gottfried had visited Bryce Cameron's cabin, and he knew generally where it was located. To the best of his memory it was on the west shore of Lake Clark, about ten miles from his current position. Unfortunately, in order to get there he either had to cross Lake Clark or the Newhalen River at the outlet of the lake. Either of those options required a boat. The river was too wide and cold to feasibly swim, especially with all his gear. Max remembered that an Alaska Native community was located where the river meets the lake. He gave some thought to hiring a local resident to take him across the river or maybe all the way to Bryce's cabin. It would be a risk, but he was pretty sure that he could buy silence with enough cash. That had always worked well for him in Afghanistan.

In the morning he started hiking down from the high country toward the lake. He could see a road maybe five miles away in the distance. The road appeared to end at the river, and Max figured that it was used mostly in the winter when vehicles could cross to the village on the ice. Using his binoculars, he could also see two boats pulled up on shore near the end of the road. It seemed logical that someone would be coming for the boats eventually. He could probably steal one, but it might be better to contact the owner and get a ride. A stolen boat might lead to a manhunt, so Max decided he would just head that way and play it by ear. The remainder of the day was spent traversing bogs and woodlands. He camped in spruce forest close to the landing area at the end of the road but far enough away to be well out of sight.

†

"So, what's going on with Karelian?" asked JB as he helped himself to yet another cup of Charlie's coffee.

"He still seems to be in the wind," replied the Super Trooper. "There's no sign of him anywhere. He's either still wandering around in the mountains, or he's figured out a way to get back to civilization."

"Are we sure that he is the murderer?" asked Kate.

"Circumstantial evidence is pretty strong. Also, his fingerprints were found on the radiation meter and the field books taken from the South Peninsula Gold campsite. Travis Chen's prints were also found on the meter, but some of them were on top of Karelian's, suggesting that Max handled it first," said Bob.

The three mooseketeers plus Beverly were spending another Saturday morning in the cabin of the Shearwater. Bob had dropped by to give them an update on the NBM investigation. The bright morning sun was warming the cabin, creating a welcome coziness. The shorter daylight of late summer was a harbinger of fall, bringing cooler nights and changeable weather. As usual, the cozy atmosphere of the Shearwater's galley was enhanced by a plate of cinnamon rolls, abundant coffee, and a purring cat lounging on Kate's lap. It seemed like discussions of murders had become commonplace, given the events of the past three years. The dual romances between Kate and Charlie and JB and Beverly, spawned by mutual interests in dead bodies three years before, seemed to be holding fast.

"So, what's happening with the investigation?" asked JB.

"I'm not really sure. It's pretty much out of the troopers' hands at this point. The FBI and CIA are working with Canadian authorities to investigate the NBM corporate structure and the people behind the whole idea. The troopers are still in charge of the manhunt for Max, but there are currently no leads."

"Is there anything we can do to help?" asked Kate.

"As always, I'm open to suggestions," replied Bob, his mouth full of pastry.

"I've been giving some thought to what Karelian might be doing," JB said as he reached for another roll. "Since he didn't go back to the camp and no one has seen him for over two weeks, it seems reasonable that he is still wandering around in the bush somewhere. I suppose he could have gotten himself into trouble somehow, but he struck me as being skilled and resourceful, so I doubt it. So, if he's still wandering around, what might his end game be? He can't stay out there forever. It's going to get cold soon. Most likely he is going to try and find a way back to civilization without being conspicuous. What do you guys think his plan may be?"

"The geography limits his options. He would have to go south and west from the NBM camp to go around the mountains. It might be possible to get to the Lake Clark area, but it would be a difficult hike. But, let's assume he does get near Lake Clark, then what would he do?" Charlie responded.

Kate pulled up Google Earth on her laptop as they were talking. "Coming from the east in a logical path would take him to the south end of the lake. There may be some cabins in the area, plus the village of Nondalton is located near the lake outlet on the north side. He could somehow cross the lake or river to Nondalton and get help from there, or he could walk about twenty miles up the east side of the lake to Port Alsworth, where there is an airstrip."

"Port Alsworth has regular air service and communications with the outside world, so residents almost certainly are aware of Karelian's fugitive status," added Charlie. "On the other hand, Nondalton is somewhat more isolated, both culturally and physically. If I were Max, I would try to pay off someone in the village to help out. But what kind of help would he be looking for? I don't think there are any planes in the village, but there are lots of boats."

"When we talked to Bryce Cameron, the investor with the cabin on Lake Clark, he mentioned that Karelian was present when he met with the NBM guys," JB said. "So Karelian may know where Cameron's cabin is located. I suspect Cameron could be easily intimidated by Karelian. Plus Cameron's airplane would be the perfect getaway transportation. Even if Cameron isn't there, the cabin would be a good place to get temporary refuge."

"Is Cameron aware that Karelian may be wandering around in the wilderness?" asked Charlie.

"He was questioned by trooper investigators and the FBI, but I don't know whether they warned him about the possibility of contact with Karelian. Also, I don't know whether he is still living at the cabin or in Anchorage," replied Bob.

"Can you try and find out?" Charlie asked Bob.

"I can call his wife right now. She may know where he is," said Bob as he looked in his phone contacts and dialed, putting the phone on speaker so that the others could hear. The phone was answered after two rings.

"Mrs. Cameron, this is Bob Stillwater of the state troopers. We're worried about your husband and wondered if you know where he is – is he still at his Lake Clark cabin?"

"He was in Anchorage for a couple of weeks but just went back to the cabin yesterday. What's going on?"

"Is there some way we can contact him?"

"There's no phone service, but he sometimes communicates by marine VHF radio. He calls someone in Port Alsworth and they relay messages by satphone."

"Can it be used the other way around?" asked Bob.

"I guess so if they have their radios on. Is Bryce in some kind of danger? It has something to do with the mine project that was raided, doesn't it?"

"Yeah. We're afraid that one of the fugitives from the mine may try to contact Bryce and force him to fly him out."

"Oh, crap. I would try to reach him but I don't know who to call," said Mrs. Cameron.

"We'll see if we can find a way to contact him and let you know if we do," Bob replied as he ended the call.

Charlie knew that communication by marine radio, while technically illegal for strictly land-based activities, was often used in remote areas in Alaska where the radio traffic would not interfere with legitimate marine uses. Authorities generally looked the other way, especially for emergency needs. The range of VHF radios was limited to line of sight, maybe twenty miles depending on antenna height and geographical barriers.

As Bob was getting up to leave the Shearwater, he indicated that he would go back to his office and try to reach someone in Port Alsworth.

Chapter Twenty-Nine

Bryce Cameron filled a glass with two fingers of Jack Daniels and reclined on the chaise lounge on the front porch of his cabin overlooking the lake. The sun glinted off the glaciers across the lake, and the amazing turquoise water contrasted with the darker green of the trees. He was thinking that his life might be on a badly needed upward trajectory. The last two weeks had been seriously stressful. He had been interviewed for twelve hours by various law enforcement officials and had spent many hours in his lawyer's office discussing strategy for avoiding prosecution and maybe even getting some of his money back from NBM. Apparently, he successfully convinced the Feds that the only thing he was guilty of was stupidity. On the positive side, it looked like his wife was softening her opinion of him. They had some good discussions, and he felt optimistic that she would take him back. They decided that he should take a few days to get his head together and then return to Anchorage.

He watched the sun dip behind the mountains and immediately felt a chill in the air, so he retreated inside and started a fire. He poured another drink and began to sit down when the radio crackled, and he heard a voice calling his name.

What the heck?

He responded to the call and discovered that it was someone from the Port Alsworth airstrip relaying a message from the state troopers that he should be on the lookout for a fugitive named Max Karelian who may want to hijack his plane. The vague message sounded urgent but provided no details of the potential danger. His buoyant mood suddenly shattered. He had met Max in the early NBM meetings and found him to be creepy and intimidating. He tried to reason what his next steps should be, in spite of the fact that his brain was clouded by a sense of panic. Flying to Anchorage right away was out of the question – darkness was arriving fast and he could see clouds obscuring the mountain passes at the north end of the lake. The mountainous terrain between Lake Clark and Anchorage was littered with wrecked planes. He would have to wait until at least the next day. Bryce locked the doors and windows and retrieved a rifle that had not been fired in years. Pretending he was not there was pointless since his airplane was parked at the dock.

†

Mid-morning the following day, Nicholas John drove his ancient Datsun pickup slowly along the gravel road that led from Iliamna to its end at the river across from the village of Nondalton. The various rattles were so loud that he could barely hear the country music blaring from an old tape player. Like many Athabascan men, Nicholas was short and wiry, the muscles and tendons standing out in sharp relief on his arms. His face was handsome in a rugged, weathered sort of way, and his long black hair was tied back in a ponytail.

The bed of the truck was filled with boxes of groceries and other supplies ordered from the Costco store in Anchorage and delivered by air freight to Iliamna, the closest village freight hub. Nicholas made four of these trips each year to supply his family with essentials, supplementing the local subsistence food supply of salmon, moose, berries, and limited produce from a vegetable garden. He pulled into the parking area at road's end and began hauling the heavy boxes down a steep bank to his boat, which was pulled up on a gravel bar at the edge of the wide river. The process would have to be repeated in reverse on the other side of the river where he would carry boxes up a bank to his four-wheel ATV, his primary transport in the village. Nicholas then had to haul the boxes from the ATV into his small house. He was looking forward to the day when his five-year-old son could help with this chore.

As he reached into the truck for his second load, he spotted a large hairy, dirty white man dressed in camouflage emerging from the forest and walking toward him. He had an automatic pistol in a holster on his hip and carried a substantial backpack. Nicholas was an easy going, friendly guy but was naturally suspicious of the stranger.

"Where the hell did you come from?" said Nicholas as he tried to assess the man's motives.

"I'm on a hike from the coast and I need to get to a friend's house on the west shore of Lake Clark."

Nicholas thought about that, taking his time in the manner common to Alaska Natives. "You walked all the way from the coast? Why would you do that?"

"I like challenges. My friend has a cabin about ten miles up the lake from here. I'd be glad to pay someone willing to take me there by boat."

"OK. How much would you pay?"

"How about two hundred dollars?"

"Sounds good on one condition. You need to help me haul these fuckin' boxes to my house."

"I can do that."

"What's your friend's name?"

"Bryce Cameron."

"I know where his place is. Should be no problem. By the way, I'm

Nicholas."

"Just call me Max."

"We don't get many white men visitors to Nondalton, except teachers and government workers. You are pretty unusual."

"I'd appreciate it if we didn't attract too much attention. For various reasons, I'd like to stay out of sight," replied Max.

They started hauling groceries to the flat-bottomed aluminum johnboat powered by a fifty-horsepower outboard motor. Max was skeptical that the boat would hold the weight, but there seemed to be no problem. After crossing the wide river to a landing at the other side, they moved boxes onto a trailer attached to a dirty, beat-up ATV. Max rode behind Nicholas on the motorcycle-type seat. The dirt road that served as the village main street was lined with scattered small houses, a small general store, and a more modern looking government building. The village appeared to be mostly deserted, and few people took notice of Max's presence.

As they approached Nicholas's cabin, his attractive partner stepped out on the front porch to see what was going on. "Max, this is my wife, Betty. Betty, this is Max. He's helping with the food boxes in exchange for a ride to Bryce Cameron's place on the lake."

"Well, thanks Max," said Betty.

"My pleasure," replied Max as he took a good look at Betty's glossy long dark hair and pretty face. The sight of the first woman he had seen in several weeks caused his mind to involuntarily wander to places he did not want it to go. He had too many other things to think about.

Max continued his helpful neighbor act until the boxes were all neatly stacked in the kitchen. When they were done, Nicholas retrieved a full gas can from his storage shed, and they returned to the boat. Soon they were roaring up river and into Lake Clark. The water was reasonably calm and the overpowered sixteen-foot boat was streaking over the surface of the lake at about thirty-five knots.

†

Bryce was running through the forest soaked with sweat, stalked by a large, swarthy man in dark clothes wielding a large black pistol. Small, stiff branches from underbrush kept whipping him in the face, and he kept tripping over tree roots. Bryce suddenly sat up in bed. It slowly dawned on him that he was dreaming, and what was worse, the dream had elements of truth. He needed to get the hell out of there. He got dressed and immediately ran out to his dock to get a good view of the cloud conditions in the passes at the head of the lake. It still looked like it was socked in. *Crap.* He would not be going anywhere by airplane for a while. He decided to wait until mid-morning when the clouds normally cleared. If he still could not fly, he would take his boat across the lake to Port Alsworth. Presumably, Max Karelian would not pursue him there. Of course, if Max happened to have a pilot's license and floatplane experience, he could just steal the plane. To Bryce that seemed unlikely.

He busied himself by preparing the cabin for a prolonged absence, packed his duffel bag for an immediate departure, and began hauling stuff to his plane. By mid-afternoon the clouds had still not cleared. While on the dock he heard a faint sound of an outboard motor coming from the south end of the lake. The lake was calm and quiet and any sounds on its surface traveled a long way. Boats were not unusual, but Bryce's paranoia kicked in and he reached into the cockpit of the plane for his binoculars. He was able to see a small boat more than a mile away. It looked like there were two people in the boat but they were much too far to make out any details. But they were heading directly for his cabin and moving fast.

Fuck it, I'm getting out of here while I can. He ran back to the cabin, got the plane keys, locked the cabin door, ran back to the dock, jumped into his plane, and prayed that it would start right away. Fortunately the engine fired right up. In the midst of his panic, Bryce realized that he had almost forgotten to untie the plane from the dock. Jumping back out of the plane, he untied the lines and pushed off onto the float. Back in the cockpit, he revved the engine and taxied into open water. The approaching boat was about a quarter mile away. He had to go right now. Without waiting for the engine to warm up completely, Bryce powered to takeoff speed and lifted off the lake surface, flying directly over the boat. Banking to the right, he was able to get a good look at the occupants. He saw that the driver was probably native and the passenger was a large man dressed in camo with a full black beard. He had little doubt — the passenger was Max Karelian.

Bryce gained altitude and flew south where the weather looked better. He contacted flight control and asked them to relay a message to the state troopers that the fugitive, Max Karelian, was likely near his cabin on Lake Clark and that Bryce would be landing on Beluga Lake in Homer in about an hour. The controller passed the message to Bob Stillwater, who indicated that he would meet the plane on arrival to get details.

Much to Bryce's relief, visibility was reasonably good all the way to Homer. He landed without incident. The Super Trooper was standing at the general aviation dock to meet him. With him were Charlie Skyler, JB Bachman, and another woman introduced as Beverly.

†

Max Karelian was helpless as he watched Bryce Cameron run to his plane and take off. They were five minutes too late. Nicholas John slowed the boat to idle as the plane flew overhead.

"I think you missed your friend. What do you want to do now?" Nicholas asked.

Max let loose a string of expletives and Nicholas began to realize that the occupant of the plane might not actually be a friend.

"Take me to the dock," said Max. He got out of the boat with his gear and told Nicholas to leave him.

"Where's my money?" asked Nicholas.

Because of his frustrated state of mind, Max's first impulse was to pull his gun and tell his companion to get lost, but, on second thought, he decided that minimizing conflict might be a better strategy. He grabbed a wad of bills from inside his jacket, counted out two hundred dollars and held it just out of reach.

"Keep your mouth shut. I'm not here," Max said.

"No problem. I was never here either," replied Nicholas as he grabbed the money. "But I think your friend already knows you're here."

Nicholas pushed off and headed for home as fast as he could go, relieved to be out of range of Max's pistol. Max walked to the cabin, broke the latch on the front door, made himself comfortable on Bryce's leather couch, and tried to figure out his next move. He was not completely sure whether Bryce would call the authorities or not. He had not been privy to arrangements between Bryce and his bosses, so was not sure the extent of Cameron's involvement with the illegal enterprise. However, if Max could guess, it was certainly possible that Bryce would call the cops. In any event, he figured it would be a while before anyone pursued him at this remote location, especially since it was starting to get dark.

Meanwhile, he was very hungry and tired of living off the land.

It looked like Bryce had taken most of the fresh food with him, but there was a well-stocked pantry of various canned foods and staples. He gorged himself on instant pancakes and fried Spam, all drenched in syrup. As a special bonus he found a bottle of high-quality bourbon, most of which he consumed while gazing out the front window at the beautiful lake.

He awoke a couple hours later with a headache and a sickening feeling that he needed to get it together before the cabin was raided. As he was restocking his backpack with provisions from Bryce's kitchen, an obvious thought hit him. He still had a functioning satellite phone, he was located on a lake where float planes could land, and he had plenty of money. Why not order a plane to come and pick him up? It was done all the time in the Alaska bush. There was even an Anchorage phone book on Bryce's desk. It was a little risky, but it would certainly be better than wandering around in the wilderness again with the cops chasing him.

Listings for bush pilots in the directory took up two pages. Max looked for a listing that suggested a small, sketchy operator who would be least likely to be concerned about legality. He settled on *Smiley's Awesome Tours*. Any company with a stupid name like that had to be sketchy. Smiley immediately answered the phone and agreed to pick Max up at seven the next morning. Max supplied coordinates from his GPS that would hopefully assure Smiley would not get lost.

That night Max Karelian took a shower and slept on a real mattress for the first time in almost a month.

Chapter Thirty

Early the next morning the small shed at Churchill Air Service on Beluga Lake was crowded. While Frank Churchill pumped fuel into his Beaver float plane from a large avgas tank on the shore, Charlie, JB, Kate, Beverly, Bob the trooper, and Bryce Cameron sat on the ratty furniture and drank bad coffee. An industrial coffee maker the size of a hot water heater chugged away in the corner. As Charlie sipped the tar-like coffee, he flashed back on all the time he had spent in similar habitats in rural Alaska. The state seemed to run on bad coffee.

The Super Trooper was conflicted about bringing civilians on an obvious manhunt. He had tried to enlist help from the law enforcement community, but no one was available on short notice. He figured he did not have much choice since he needed backup and the mooseketeers were already familiar with the situation. In actuality, he was more comfortable with the guys from Homer than some of his trooper colleagues.

"What are you guys going to do when you get to Cameron's cabin?" asked Kate.

"I guess we won't know until we get there. If no one's home we'll look around and see what we can see. If Karelian is there we'll go after him," replied Charlie.

"What if he shoots at you?"

"We'll approach carefully. If he shoots, we'll shoot back," replied Bob.

"I'm guessing that Frank doesn't want holes in his airplane," said

JB. "It might be wise to land down the shore and approach the cabin on foot."

"Sounds like a plan," said Bob.

Frank Churchill stuck his head into the shed. "I guess we're ready to go."

All but Kate climbed aboard the plane. "Why do I always get to hold down the fort?" grumbled Kate.

The flight to Lake Clark was uneventful. Bob asked the pilot to fly high over the cabin. Cameron's boat was still at the dock, so obviously Max Karelian had not left by water. They flew down the lake out of sight of the cabin and landed the plane at a neighbor's cabin in a bay a half mile away. Churchill gave Bob a mobile radio so that he could summon the plane if needed.

Charlie, JB, Beverly, Bob, and Bryce began walking through the trees along the shoreline. The terrain was flat and the forest understory was sparse, so walking was reasonably easy and fast. They figured they would be at Bryce's cabin in about ten minutes.

†

Max Karelian woke at sunrise, feeling refreshed after his night on the plush king-sized mattress. He fixed himself a big breakfast of instant pancakes and canned sausages, packed his stuff, and got ready to meet the plane from *Smiley's Awesome Tours*. While waiting, Max relaxed on the chaise lounge on the front porch. The sun was starting to appear over the mountains, warming an already warm morning. Small fish, maybe baby salmon, were rising and dimpling the smooth surface of the water. It seemed like a good omen of things to come.

Max sat up as he heard the sound of a plane approaching from the north – Smiley was right on time. A red Cessna 180 float plane cruised past the cabin, then banked, turned, and landed smoothly in the calm bay. Smiley taxied to the dock as Max grabbed his backpack and ran to meet him.

"You must be Max," said Smiley.

"Don't bother to shut down. We need to get out of here," Max said.

"What's your hurry? It's beautiful day," asked Smiley.

"I'm on a tight schedule. Let's get going."

Smiley opened the rear door of the Cessna and Max transferred the heavy pack from the dock to the plane.

Suddenly, the sound of a gunshot reverberated off the mountain sides.

"What the fuck was that?" asked Smiley.

Max looked down the shore and saw four men and a woman running toward them, one of whom was in a trooper uniform. They were yelling but could not be heard over the sound of the airplane engine.

"It's the cops. I better wait."

"Not on your life," Max growled as he pulled the Glock from under his jacket and pointed it at Smiley's head. "Into the plane right now."

"Shit," said Smiley as he leaped into the pilot seat with Max right behind.

"Go. Go!" Max yelled with a wave of his gun.

The plane pulled away just as the four men reached the dock, and in a minute they were airborne.

"I get the feeling you're not an upstanding citizen. So where do we go now, especially since all the airports are probably going to be alerted to look for us?" asked Smiley.

"That is sort of a problem," answered Max. "I'm counting on you to figure out a place we can land where no one can see us and I can slip away. Your life may depend on it."

"There are wilderness lakes all over the place, but you would end up stranded again."

"Yeah. You're smarter than you look. We need to find a place secluded enough for a drop off but close enough to transportation systems so I can get out of the state."

"Obviously, we're limited by fuel. We can only go so far before we fall out of the sky. One possibility might be the northern Kenai Peninsula. There are many small wilderness lakes, some of which would be in hiking distance of roads. I think I can get there without arousing suspicion."

Smiley pulled a map out of his pilot's case and pointed to a likely destination. A maze of roads led to the community of Soldotna located on the main road to Anchorage. Max would have to do some hiking, but what's a few more miles?

"How long would it take to get there?"

"Probably less than an hour."

"Does this plane have a tracking device?"

"No, my business isn't exactly booming, so bells and whistles are limited."

"Excellent. Please give me your mobile phone."

"Really?" Smiley looked at the big black pistol. He reluctantly fished out the phone from his pocket and handed it to Max, who promptly threw it out the window.

The little plane cleared the north end of Lake Clark, turned east through a maze of rugged mountain spires, and approached Cook Inlet, ironically nearly passing over the mine camp where Max had started his long trek. The plane reached the mine camp area in about fifteen minutes in contrast to the three weeks spent by Max on foot.

Crossing the inlet to the Kenai Peninsula, Smiley skirted the population centers along the Kenai River, entered the Kenai National Wildlife Refuge from the east, and then flew west to an area dotted with small lakes.

"I suggest you look out the window to get some idea of where the roads go. I'm going to land on the lake directly ahead of us and drop you off on the south shore, which is about a half mile from the nearest road. I'm a little concerned about what might happen after we land since I am a witness to your location and could report it. Obviously, I'd rather not get shot. I noticed from your tattoo that you have spent time in Afghanistan. I was a chopper pilot in Helmand. I promise as a fellow vet that I won't report you. What happens now is up to you," said Smiley.

"I'll keep that in mind," Max said. At that moment he had actually been thinking about what to do with Smiley. He had to admire how cool the guy was, and he had been pretty helpful. *What the hell, I'm in enough trouble already. I don't need to kill anyone else.*

The little plane descended to a smooth landing and taxied to within a few feet of the shore. "You may have to get your feet wet," Smiley remarked as he handed the heavy pack to Max. Max jumped off the float into knee deep water and turned toward shore.

"Get the hell out of here and keep your mouth shut," yelled Max.

"Roger that," Smiley replied. The plane taxied clear of the shore and took off immediately. To say that Smiley was relieved would be an understatement.

†

Charlie and the gang emerged from the woods at the edge of Bryce's property just in time to see Max Karelian load his pack into the plane.

Bob fired a shot in the air in an attempt to alert the passengers and hopefully stop the plane from leaving. They ran across the lawn, but they were just too late. The red plane accelerated away from the dock as they raced down the pier. Charlie wrote the tail number on the back of his hand, and Bob radioed Frank Churchill to immediately bring his plane around to Cameron's. By the time the Churchill Air Service plane reached Bryce's dock, the red Cessna, presumably containing Max Karelian, was out of sight.

Charlie, JB, Beverly, and Bob quickly boarded the Churchill plane, and the Beaver took off and headed in the direction of the red Cessna. Bryce elected to stay at the cabin to check on things. Once in the air, Bob commandeered the aviation radio to call in the tail number of the fugitive plane. A few minutes later he got a response indicating that the plane belonged to *Smiley's Awesome Tours* out of Merrill Field in Anchorage. Bob asked the controller to call Smiley's and let them know that their plane probably had been hijacked by a fugitive and to put out an all-points bulletin within the range of the small plane.

While Bob was dealing with communications, Frank gained as much altitude as he could. Fortunately, the sky was totally clear and he was able to safely navigate the mountains on all sides. As they cleared the north end of Lake Clark and the mountains, the vista opened up and they were able to see far across Cook Inlet to the Kenai Peninsula and beyond.

"I think I see them," said Charlie, pointing to a red speck far to the east.

"I've got it," Frank Churchill said as he banked right and headed for the central portion of the Kenai Peninsula, with the red Cessna about fifteen miles dead ahead.

They flew toward the early morning sun with Cook Inlet glinting silver-grey like rippled mercury below them. Several offshore oil rigs and their natural gas flares were visible to the north. Many commercial fishing boats were scattered across the watery expanse below them. These small "drift gill netters" caught fish by drifting in the current with monofilament nets trailing behind, hoping to intercept a school of sockeye salmon on its way to the productive Kenai River. The water in Cook Inlet was multicolored – milky gray water from glacial drainages, turquoise green water from rivers originating from lakes, and clear marine water from the Gulf of Alaska, all mixed by the chaotic tides.

"It looks like they're turning north," observed Frank as they approached the west shore of the inlet. "My guess is that they're trying to avoid population centers around Kenai and Anchorage. We can gain some distance by shortcutting the jog in their route."

"Do you think they can see us?" asked JB.

"Probably not. Visibility to the rear of a plane is pretty much nonexistent. I doubt the Cessna has radar."

"Let's keep following them. Do whatever you need to do to not get in trouble with aviation authorities," Bob said.

Frank Churchill reported in to air traffic control that they were following a plane possibly carrying a fugitive. He anticipated the trajectory of the Cessna and headed northeast to where he figured their paths would intersect, and hopefully reduce the distance between them. They crossed the Kenai River as well as the linear highway town of Soldotna and headed toward the Kenai Wildlife Refuge, closing the distance from the red Cessna to within a few miles. Churchill then resumed his position directly behind the subject plane out of their field of view. In a few minutes it became obvious that the Cessna was descending and aiming for one of the many small lakes in the vicinity.

"Let's hold back and see where they land without spooking them," suggested JB.

"Roger that," Frank said as he banked right.

They watched as the Cessna landed on the lake and dropped off a passenger. The red plane immediately took off and headed north toward Anchorage.

"Report our position and ask for backup on the nearest roads, then land where they landed," Bob said.

The Churchill Air Service Beaver landed on the small lake about ten minutes after the Cessna, taxied to the shore, and disgorged its passengers into the shallow water at the lake margin.

Chapter Thirty-One

Max discovered right away that it was not going to be fun. The terrain at the edge of the lake was low lying and swampy. The ground was hummocky and squishy, covered by woody shrubs and sphagnum moss with occasional islands of higher ground forested by birch and spruce, sort of like a subarctic Everglades. His heavy backpack interfered with maintaining balance on the irregular ground. The past weeks of wandering the wilderness had prepared him mentally and physically to deal with adverse conditions, but he was in a bad mood and cursed every time he fell to his knees or went up to his thighs in cold water. He had heard the sounds of an airplane landing and taking off from the lake behind him. Somehow, the people at Cameron's cabin must have followed him, but he did not really understand how it was possible that they could be so close.

His GPS mapping device showed a road about a half mile to the south, but the fact that there were people behind him suggested that the roads might also be patrolled. Max Karelian was in a quandary as to what to do. He figured that tracking him might be pretty easy in the swampy areas because each step left an impression as well as a wisp of dirty water. Tracking on high ground would be more difficult. He concluded that hiding for a while in a good defensive position might be the best option, if he could find a good spot. He looked at the satellite map on his GPS and identified a small stream with a forested ridge on its far side. The stream was maybe a quarter mile from his present position. He began slogging toward the stream.

Twenty minutes later he reached the shallow waterway. Moderate current and a gravel bottom seemed promising for covering his tracks – signs of his presence would be washed away in minutes. He first crossed the stream and climbed onto its bank, then carefully walked backwards back into the stream. He hoped to confuse his pursuers into thinking that he had gone straight across. He walked downstream in the water for several hundred yards, then carefully climbed the bank in a shrubby area, thus minimizing traces of his passage. Once he was on the high ground across the stream, walking was easier in the birch forest, and his footsteps left little sign in the dry forest duff. Near the top of the ridge the trees thinned out and rock outcrops were exposed. The area looked promising as a hideout as well as a good defensive position. Max crawled into a niche between boulders, laid out his limited weaponry, and waited to see what might happen.

†

Charlie, JB, Beverly, and the Super Trooper exited the plane and gathered on shore near the location where they thought Max Karelian had headed overland.

"It looks like he came ashore here," JB said as he waded along the shoreline.

"OK. So, how are we gonna work this?" asked Bob.

"I think I can probably track him," replied JB. "The problem is he could wait somewhere and pick us off one by one. I suggest we spread out with me in the middle on the trail and you guys about twenty feet away on each side. That way he won't go shooting us all at once."

"On that optimistic note, I guess we should get going," said Charlie.

The four pursuers began moving slowly through the wetlands

adjacent to the lake shore. It was deceptively peaceful. The pungent smell of Labrador tea mixed with the cloying smell of sweet gale. Hints of hydrogen sulfide added to the mix as footsteps in the ooze released marsh gas. Buzzing of bees, mosquitoes, and flies created white noise in the background.

The pace was limited by JB's ability to pick up Max's trail. Tracking was slow but mostly pretty easy. Occasionally the signs disappeared and JB had to double back to find the trail again. They plodded forward quietly. Moving through the lumpy terrain was exhausting, similar to hiking through deep snow. The wet sphagnum and muck sucked onto boots increasing the effort of each step. After about fifteen minutes, they regrouped to look at satellite images of the terrain in relation to their current location.

"I assume Max has a GPS mapping device like ours. It looks like he is heading for the high ground southeast of here and may try to take advantage of the stream shown on the map to make us lose the trail. That's what I would do if I were him. We need to be careful from now on," said JB.

Ten minutes later they reached the stream. JB crossed and climbed up the far bank. Returning to the group he said, "I think he is trying to spoof us into thinking that he went straight across. So, the next question is, did he go upstream or downstream? Any ideas?"

"I vote for downstream," Charlie said. "Silt kicked up by walking on the stream bottom would wash immediately downstream and not give him away to pursuers standing upstream where we are. But, on the other hand, we're probably almost a half hour behind him, so disturbance upstream might have also washed away already."

"Downstream it is," replied JB. "Let's go." The group started walking downstream in the water, while JB surveyed the right bank for signs of someone leaving the stream and heading toward the higher ground. Schools of humpback salmon frantically tried to avoid the big feet invading their domain. After a couple hundred yards, JB spotted a clump of willows that looked like they might have been parted to allow passage. A careful look on the bank beyond the willows suggested recent disturbance.

"Here we go," said JB. "Let's get back into our staggered pursuit mode."

Once again following Max Karelian's trail, the intrepid group plodded through the forest up the gentle hillside they had seen on the maps. The mixed birch-spruce forest on the upland made for easier walking, but it was more open than the swamp from which they had recently emerged. The greater visibility meant that they could be seen more easily. After about ten minutes they were able to see the ridge top and rock outcroppings above them through the trees. JB signaled for Bob and Charlie to stop and find cover while he scouted the terrain ahead of them.

†

While Max was waiting in his nest between the rocks, he peered out into the forest below. He looked down onto the line of trees at the toe of the slope and saw no movement other than a squirrel. The only sound was that of leaves rustling in the breeze and a few distant bird calls. He began to relax. Maybe his pursuers had lost his trail and were floundering around in the trackless woods. He could always hope. Max started to think about how he might be able to escape his current predicament. One possibility was hiking to the highway, getting a ride from someone on the way to Anchorage, and flying out of state from there. He had false identity documents in his pack and figured he could alter his appearance enough to prevent the airport authorities from recognizing him based on wanted photos.

Another possibility would be to somehow get to Seward and hitch a ride on a fishing boat to the lower forty-eight. He was tired of the whole damn thing and wondering how he could have been so stupid as to get involved with the NWB project in the first place. Of course, Max knew that the answer came down to money. Greed always seemed to win out during his decision processes. But, in this case, he had spent nearly a month wandering around in the Alaskan wilderness and had little to show for it, except perhaps a more philosophical view of his violent life to date.

Max again peeked around the corner of his rock shelter and saw a movement in the trees. Looking further, he noticed movement in two places. *Shit. How do they keep finding me?* Realizing that it was do-or-die time, he put aside the optimistic thoughts of the previous few minutes and resumed his normal fatalistic outlook. *Well, here we go.* Max propped his little rifle on a dirt mound and aimed carefully. He could see the tall hippy guy crouched behind a spruce that was not quite big enough to hide his whole body. He fired and knew that the shot came close to the target but was unable to tell whether he had actually hit anything. Shifting his sights to the right, he saw another body and fired but, again, was not sure whether he had done any damage.

†

As the four pursuers regrouped and planned their next moves, a shot from a small caliber weapon surprised them all, and splinters of tree bark hit JB in the face.

"Holy shit that was close!" whispered JB. Another shot from a different caliber followed. This time tree bark was shredded over a larger area and rained down on Charlie's head. Obviously, the shooter was able to see both of them even though they were ten yards apart and crouched behind trees. But they weren't able to see the shooter.

"He's hiding up in the rocks and we're sitting ducks right now!" yelled Beverly as everyone scrambled to get behind the biggest tree they could find. Unfortunately, most of the trees were less than twelve inches in diameter.

"The gunshots are a little confusing," added JB. "The first was a .22 and the second was a small-caliber shotgun. One possibility is that he has one of those little over-and-under survival guns. If that's the case then he only has one shot from each barrel before reloading. We have to assume that he also still has his Glock."

"OK, so what do we do now? The signal on my phone is marginal. I can't get a call through right now," asked Bob.

"I guess we're on our own. Let's see if the phone signal is strong enough to text so we can communicate with each other," Charlie said. A quick test of texting indicated that it would likely be possible.

"We need to first pinpoint his location and then try to get behind him. He's obviously going to be expecting that since it's our only move right now other than retreating. Let me move back out of sight, then over to the right and see if I can get a better view of the rocks. I'll text you if I see anything useful," replied JB. "Meanwhile, lay low and don't take any chances."

JB slithered on his stomach back from Max Karelian's apparent viewpoint, then moved sideways from tree to tree until he was about a hundred yards away from the others. Carefully approaching the ridge once again, he was able to get a somewhat different perspective and picked out at least one possible location for Max's hiding spot.

He texted to Charlie and Bob:

Looking at 2 flat rock faces with scraggly leaning spruce on rt. side. Fire two shots at side of left rock so that ricochet goes between the rocks. Maybe we'll get a response.

Bob fired his service pistol at the rock and immediately ducked. A few seconds later Max fired two shots from his survival rifle at the place where Bob had been seconds before.

OK. We know where he is. I'm going to work my way around to the side. If you hear any shots, return fire to the same location to distract him.

JB emerged from the trees and began to climb the ridge. Although he was now quite visible, he was pretty sure Max couldn't see him in his current location. Nevertheless, he ran as fast as he could to some boulders near the ridgetop. Back in slither mode, he oozed around the boulder field to see if he could get a glimpse of Max's sniper nest. Peeking around a rock he thought he could see a foot sticking out from the back corner of a large outcrop. Binoculars confirmed that it was indeed a booted foot protruding about eight inches beyond his rock cover. Unfortunately, he was much too far to chance a shot at such a small target with his little pocket Beretta.

Have spotted him but too far away to get a shot. I'm going to move up closer. When you hear shots, approach Karelian's location from two angles while giving covering fire. Hopefully he won't be able to shoot in three directions at once. Please don't shoot me.

JB moved closer, darting from rock to rock. He expected that Max would stand up and look to the side any minute in anticipation of a flanking maneuver. But JB managed to make it unseen to a larger boulder with a blueberry bush growing alongside. Peering through the branches, he could see the protruding foot. It was still a long shot, but JB rested his arm on the ground, aimed carefully, and fired two shots. The shots were followed immediately by a scream which was followed by four quick shots from downhill, obviously from Bob's Glock. A louder boom from Charlie's shotgun was followed by two shots from Max's survival rifle.

JB took advantage of the confusion and gunfire to move closer. He caught a brief glimpse of Max's head as he crept around and saw a hand holding a pistol emerge over the rock face and fire two blind shots in his direction. With a tree providing partial cover, JB raised his gun and waited for another opportunity. More shots were fired from downhill. Max again peeked over the rock and aimed in JB's direction. As Max's hand came into view, JB fired two more shots. Another scream and the hand disappeared.

"Max Karelian, you're under arrest!" yelled Bob from downhill but much closer than before. There was no answer. JB moved to the big rock, looked around the corner and saw Max on the ground moaning and holding a bloody hand while even more blood trickled out of his ankle. The pieces of a mangled pistol lay on the ground along with the rifle, which was broken open and unloaded.

"Don't move," ordered JB.

"How can I move? You've fucked up my foot."

"It's safe to come up," JB yelled to Charlie, Beverly, and Bob, and all assembled around the whimpering mercenary.

"OK, now what do we do?" asked Charlie. "It would be a lot easier to get out of here if you hadn't shot Max in the foot."

"Yeah, yeah. We could have just let him shoot us," replied JB.

"Never fear," answered Bob. "It looks like I've got a phone signal on the ridge top."

The Super Trooper called for a helicopter to come pick them up, preferably with a medic aboard.

†

During the helicopter ride to the Kenai hospital, Max was thinking that things could have gone better, although his thoughts were somewhat fuzzy due to the shot of morphine administered by the medic. His left hand was handcuffed to the bench seat in the chopper, and his bandaged right hand hurt like hell. His bandaged left foot hurt even more. The medic had needed to cut his one hundred fifty dollar boot away from the mangled foot, and pieces of leather had been painfully removed from the bullet hole. The bullet had gone all the way through, probably damaging bones on the way. He could look forward to a hospital stay, some operations, then long jail time. Strangely, he was not really angry with his captors. As a former soldier, he respected skill, and the guys from Homer had outwitted him all through the sorry affair. On the other hand, he was pissed at his former employers for getting him into the situation to begin with. Plus, they had left him stranded in the wilderness on his own when an exfiltration would have been relatively easy.

If he hadn't been injured, he would have considered trying to escape, but that prospect seemed unlikely since he couldn't walk and needed more medical intervention. He might as well take advantage of the free medical care courtesy of the criminal justice system. He would set aside thoughts of revenge and escape until later.

Chapter Thirty-Two

"How's your foot?" asked Bob as Max Karelian was rolled back into his hospital room after waking from the first of several possible operations on his foot.

"Crappy, thank you," answered Max.

"You should feel lucky. If anyone else had shot at you they would have aimed for center mass and you might be dead. JB has a thing about not killing people."

"I don't feel particularly lucky. What's JB's story anyway? How did he become this Ninja guy? He looks like a dweeby hippy."

"JB won't talk about his past, but he's obviously had way more training than either of us. I guess he was some kind of black ops super soldier until he retired and became a university professor and eventually a boat bum."

"Great. Just my luck."

"So, Max, did you kill the two geologists?" asked Bob. "Before you answer, you should know that we have your prints on the radiation meter and field notebooks taken from their camp. Plus, your Glock is being tested as we speak to see if the bullet taken from Jason Biele's body was fired from your gun."

"I'm not going to volunteer any information until I have a lawyer and a better idea of what's going on with my former employers."

"The Canadian authorities are dealing with the illicit activities of Northwest Base Metals. I think Lee Chen may have disappeared.

Other than that, I don't know what's going on, but I think you can assume that Northwest Base Metals is toast. The lawyer that NBM sent up here to keep Travis Chen from blabbing too much has skipped town, so I suspect you will be on your own."

"What happened to Travis Chen?"

"Travis is in jail. I can't discuss details of his case. I'll put your request for a lawyer into the system and be back for more questions later. Meanwhile, enjoy the painkillers, and don't go anywhere."

†

In fact, Travis Chen at that moment was in an interview room facing a foursome from the Vancouver Police Department Investigations Division and the RCMP. An FBI official from the Seattle, Washington, office was also sitting in as a courtesy, since the overall conspiracy involved both nations. Negotiations between Alaskan and Canadian authorities had resulted in the extradition of Travis back to his home city with the understanding that Travis had agreed to be a cooperating witness.

Travis was doing his best to provide information on the Chinese connection. However, much was unknown about how the plot originated and who had ordered it. All the information to date indicated that Lee Chen was a bitter and ambitious man and wanted to make a name for himself regardless of how many corners he had to cut. It was clear that Chinese mining and government interests had wanted to get a foothold into the rare earth metal market in the U.S., but they were insisting that Lee Chen operated on his own. Given the secrecy of the Chinese government and the Chinese underworld, it was unlikely that the plot would ever be completely unraveled.

†

In spite of Travis's cooperation, Canadian authorities had had no luck locating Lee Chen. Airports in southwestern British Columbia and northwestern Washington were being monitored, but no one using the name Lee Chen, or resembling Lee Chen, had departed in the previous weeks. Records found in Lee's office and home had provided no clues to his whereabouts. Authorities were at a dead end.

Meanwhile Lee was going crazy from boredom and frustration. Everything he had built was falling apart, and somehow his new identity made him feel that he was untethered from reality. The ski chalet was comfortable enough, but Lee was an urban person with little interest in the outdoor activities offered by the mountain retreat. On the other hand, his thirteen-year-old daughter was having a great time exploring the resort community and was looking forward to the ski season. Lee's wife, Mei, had already met other Chinese women and busied herself with games of mah-jongg. Lee Chen was becoming irrelevant to his own family. In desperation he reached out via encrypted email to colleagues in Beijing, but the few who answered asked him to cease any contact. It seemed that powerful people in the government were not happy with him or anyone connected with him. He had become a man without a country.

Another source of irritation related to the valuable objects that had been left behind in his Vancouver office. He called an underworld contact in Chinatown and asked him to discretely find out what happened to the stuff. As it turned out, the antiques had been donated to a museum, a fact that Lee found particularly galling. He had spent a lifetime accumulating his beloved artifacts, and now they were displayed in front of everybody. They were his property, and they had been stolen from him.

Lee had parked large sums of money in various offshore banks, but using any of the money without attracting attention was becoming more and more difficult because of the global emphasis on money laundering by terrorists and drug dealers. Electronic transfers had electronic records, and Canadian banks were suspicious of movements of large sums of money. Since it was not safe to fly, he could not go to offshore locations to retrieve any of the cash. Having no choice, Lee opened an account at a small Whistler bank and transferred ten thousand dollars from a bank in Panama. He hoped that it would not be flagged by the authorities because of the relatively small amount and the use of his assumed name.

The transaction probably would have gone unnoticed except that a sharp-eyed young forensic accountant in the RCMP's intelligence unit had, coincidentally, been investigating drug crimes in the Whistler area and thought the transfer was somewhat anomalous. Upon looking more carefully at the transfer recipient, he discovered that the name on the account was from a person who had died ten years earlier. He requested video from the bank's cameras and, using a facial recognition program, discovered that the bank customer was none other than Lee Chen. His discovery ultimately led to a promotion.

The Lee Chen family had laid off their body guards because they were too conspicuous and because they did not have enough money to pay them. Consequently, the local police faced no resistance and arrested Lee Chen without incident.

†

Travis Chen and his family settled into their new quarters in Halifax, Nova Scotia, about as far as you can get from Vancouver and still be in Canada. They had been outfitted with new identities and provided with a reasonable apartment in the suburbs. Travis's high-powered science education would normally have entitled him to a six-figure job, but as a person with a new name he could not lay claim to his engineering degree. This dilemma had been the subject of negotiations when he was bargaining for immunity. It was in everyone's best interest for Travis to be able to earn a living during his exile, but recreating his master's degree seemed like a reward for bad behavior. A compromise was reached where Travis would be given a fake associate degree as a geological technician, allowing him to be gainfully employed in a familiar field and, thus, cost the government less in the long run.

Much to Travis' surprise, his wife, Kathy, and seven-year-old son, Andrew, seemed to like Halifax. The sophistication of Vancouver, especially among the snobby Chinese expatriate community, had been uncomfortable for Kathy because of her Caucasian background. Andrew was enthralled by the wilds of Eastern Canada and the exciting frontier history. Tales of the voyageurs and fur trappers captivated him.

Chapter Thirty-Three

On the Saturday after the shootout, things were starting to get back to normal in the galley of the Shearwater. Charlie and Kate slept in, spending a leisurely morning under the covers of Charlie's big down sleeping bag in his teak-lined master stateroom, a miraculous space that in former days had held tons of flopping salmon. Morning activities completed, they donned sweat clothes and migrated to the galley where Charlie prepared bacon and eggs supplemented by coffee and fresh cinnamon rolls. As soon as the food hit the table, JB and Beverly emerged from the cave-like cabin of JB's sailboat and joined the party. Buster the cat assumed his preferred position between the radar display and the chart plotter on the shelf above the helm.

"So, Beverly, you really did it. You quit your job and joined the ranks of us Homeroids. Have you given more thought to your private detective idea?" asked Kate.

"Yeah. I've already applied for an Alaska PI license. I'm pretty much over-qualified so it shouldn't be a problem."

"Wow. So it looks like the three mooseketeers will now be four," added Kate as she reached for a second cinnamon roll. "What are the chances of you needing a computer nerd to help out? I'm starting to get pretty good at this sneaky hacking shit."

"I might consider that. We would make an awesome team," replied Beverly. "We could call ourselves *Otterly Ridiculous Investigations.*"

"Speaking of the *Otterly Ridiculous,* have you and JB discussed housing arrangements?" Charlie asked as he ladled scrambled eggs from a large pan.

"It's still under discussion," said JB.

"Actually, I've decided to rent a small house or cabin somewhere in town while we think about it," replied Beverly as JB exhibited an exaggerated pained expression.

"Sounds like the discussion is sort of one-sided," Kate remarked.

"Putting aside your domestic differences, I have some good news," announced Charlie. "Janine called late yesterday and said that a couple hundred pounds of core samples had been delivered to the South Peninsula Gold office. JB, do you think your professor friend would be interested in looking at the samples at minimal cost?"

"I don't see why not. He's already expressed an interest, and he has lots of captive student labor to do the job. It would be awesome if Janine could sell the claim for big bucks. There at least would be some poetic justice out of this whole sorry affair."

"Speaking of sorry affairs, Beverly, has there been any news regarding Aldo?" asked Charlie. Aldo Fenstrom was a former Kachemak Bay commercial fisherman who had been the leader of the drug distribution ring foiled by the three mooseketeers a couple of years before. He escaped to the Caribbean ahead of the law and had not been heard from since, except for a single call to JB. He was desperate for an explanation for the death of his son, Robert. The single sniper bullet that killed Robert was fired by an unknown person and was almost certainly ordered by a creepy black ops figure named Ayers. While Aldo was bent on revenge, JB convinced him that the three mooseketeers were not responsible.

"JB and I were just talking about this last night. Ayers died last winter at his home in Washington D.C. The official cause of death was a heart attack, but my old boss at the DEA made some inquiries. Some of his contacts suggested that his death might not have been totally natural. One obvious suspect in the murder would be Aldo, which may mean that he came out of exile at least long enough to avenge Robert's death. Other than that, no one knows where Aldo may be at this moment."

"Wow. That's pretty interesting," said Kate. "From what we've heard, Aldo's brother-in-law, Izzy, is using the cabin in Fenstrom's Lagoon as a summer hideaway. It would be sort of interesting to know whether he has been in touch with Aldo." Kate turned to JB.

"JB, do you think Aldo will keep his promise not to seek revenge on the four of us?"

"My feeling is that he will, but only Aldo knows for sure."

Epilogue

Janine nervously opened the letter from Professor Jackson at USC. Two weeks earlier she had shipped one hundred and fifty pounds of rock core samples to his laboratory. The university had even paid the large shipping cost.

Dear Janine,

I am very sorry for your loss. I hope things have settled down somewhat for you. Meanwhile, I have some good news. The core samples were very interesting. I will send you a complete confidential report with all the technical details, but the gist is that the property looks promising for both gold and rare earth minerals. The existence of this single core will greatly increase the value of your claim. Of course, the core is only one sample, and much more would need to be done to prove any kind of economic viability. It would probably be wise to wait and see what happens to the NBM claim in the aftermath of the summer's events. The best commercial option might be to combine the two properties, since potential buyers might want to look at them together. The fact that your claim is on tidewater is a huge benefit for future development.

I would be glad to give you advice on how to proceed with a sale of the claim. Mining is a cutthroat industry and navigating the ins and outs is not always easy. As it turns out, my students have also developed an interest in your situation, and my lab is available if you need additional analyses.

Best of luck. Feel free to give me a call any time.

- Ed

Acknowledgements

I would like to thank a number of people for their contributions to *The Rare Earth Murders*. Sara Stamey provided an initial read-through and suggested ideas for enhancement. Line editing was contributed by Haylee Graham. Proofreading was provided by Gregory Dobbin of Firefly Editing. Cover design was provided by Kathleen Weisel. Document design and file conversion was provided by Rachel Johnson.

Publication was coordinated through Village Books of Bellingham, Washington.

The excellent little book, *A History of Kachemak Bay*, by Janet Klein provided valuable historical background.